Romeo & Juliet

WILLIAM SHAKESPEARE

Romeo & Juliet

HARPER TEEN
An Imprint of HarperCollinsPublishers

HarperTeen is an imprint of HarperCollins Publishers.

Library of Congress catalog card number: 2009933427
ISBN 978-0-06-196549-4

10 11 12 13   CG / RRDH   10 9 8 7 6 5 4
❖
First HarperTeen editon, 2009

Contents

Juliet's Story:

A Retelling of William Shakespeare's
Romeo & Juliet

by Jacqueline Ritten

For my father and my mother,

You will have come for me this morning, expecting to find a bride. The guests will be gathered, the food prepared, the groom waiting. The house will be busy, expectant. The call will go up, "Juliet! Where is the girl? What, Juliet . . . ?" I have always come before. But this morning I will not.

Because I am dead.

Do not grieve. It is what I wanted.

I once had a dream that I lay with the dead. I embraced a gentleman in his shroud, laid kisses upon his cracked and yellowed skull, felt his sharp and brittle fingers at my breast. All bone, he covered me. And I was happy.

So do not grieve.

Mother, you once wished me married to my grave. That was in your rage when I said I would not marry Paris. Perhaps in some small way, then, you will be pleased by this.

That is always what I have tried to do, please you. To do your will in all things. When you called, did I not always run? "Madame, what is your will?"

Until now. Now there is another I must yield to.

Mother, Father. You who gave me life will want to know why I choose to leave it. I must try to think of you as you were, and not as I have known you for the past few days. And so you must try and remember me the same way. In our last hours together, I have told you many lies. We have said terrible things. For that I am sorry.

But even before now, you have not known my heart. Because I did not know it.

I do now. I will try to tell you what is in my heart. And I will pray that you can forgive me.

Where to begin? It has all happened so fast. A short week has been long enough to take me from maidenhood to grave.

What was my life before now? I can barely remember. Did I speak? Did you listen? All I can recall is *Yes, Father, No, Mother*, and prayers.

Nurse? I hope someone reads this letter to you. Because you will remember. You remember everything and tell the stories afterward. When I was a little girl, you told me about your childhood in the countryside, the animals and the funny people you had known. You did make me laugh.

But the stories I loved best were the ones you made up. The stories you told me of the man I would some day marry were the ones I begged to hear over and over.

"Oh, my lady shall marry a prince, who will travel far from some distant land because he heard how fair and good you are. And he shall have dark hair and blue eyes . . ." Sometimes he was blond with gray eyes. Sometimes green eyed, sometimes dark. Always tall. Always rich. He draped me in jewels and gave me palaces. And he loved me as no man had ever loved a wife.

Perhaps, Nurse, you should not have told me such love stories. Because I listened very closely.

I remember yearning for brothers and sisters, a great

romping group of children I could play with. Brothers to protect me, sisters to keep my secrets. Our house seemed too large for one small child. Once, I asked for brothers and sisters. Do you remember that, Mother? But when I did, you said it was not God's will, and something in your voice made me never ask again.

But being the only child can mean you get more. My fond, foolish, loving father, you gave me all your love, calling me your great hope in this world. Oh, you might pretend to scold and bluster. But none feared you.

I can remember crying one day because I was not a boy. You came upon me, scooped me onto your lap, and demanded to know the reason for my tears. Finally, I confessed that I was sad that you had no heir—only me. You paused a moment, then hugged me hard, saying you would want no other child but me. You were certain, you said, that I would one day marry a fine man and he would inherit all you had. But you could give him nothing more valuable than myself. Then you kissed me and said you hoped I would not marry too soon, but stay with you a bit. At this, I threw my arms around your neck and promised I would stay as long as you wanted.

Mother, you were too distant for kissing. When I think of running to you, I recall your hands held out, not to meet with mine, but to halt, hold off. As if feelings were too sharp. Kisses might scratch, hugs bruise. I can remember gazing up at you as I gazed on saints in church, anxious, hoping for favor—but uncertain that I deserved it.

Does everyone close to death think about what people will say of them afterward? It feels sinful, as if reveling in the pain we are about to cause. But I cannot turn away from such thoughts.

Nurse, you will cry loudest. I smile as I say this, because your sorrow will be noisy but sincere. Your skirt and sleeves will grow stiff from mopping up your tears. I shall leave you my handkerchiefs. And a fine new story to tell about me. Most of your stories end with laughing. But this one shall leave you sighing and weeping. "Such a fine, fair lady to be undone so!" And—confess it now—you will enjoy the tears almost as much as the laughter.

Mother—you shall be angry. Rage will be your answer to death; it always is. You and my cousin Tybalt were much alike in this. No wonder this feud between us and the Montagues has gone on for so long. Rage follows death and death follows rage and there is no end but a pile of mossy bones in a vault.

Father, I do not like to think of what you will say. Part of me prays that you remember our terrible quarrel and think, It is no bad thing to lose a child who was so ungrateful and disobedient.

When we fought, you said you did not care if I lived or died. For your sake, I hope you meant it.

In the morning, they will send you, Nurse, to wake me. You will come in, chattering as you always do. You may not even notice at first how quiet I am.

You will pull aside the bed-curtains, give my arm a shake. "Juliet, lamb! Awake now, it is your wedding day." But I will not wake. Nor move.

Your screams will draw Mother and Father. I imagine you all crowding into my chamber. Mother, Father, I can almost hear your cries: *Dead! Dead before she was married. A maiden and dead!*

But, my parents, you will be wrong. Because I am no longer a maiden. And I am already married.

Why? You will demand to know. How did this begin?

Like all the tragedies in our lives, it began with a fight. A fight that was part of this feud our family has with the Montagues. When you can tell me how this feud began, then you will have answer to why and how.

I will start with the morning of the feast.

It has been so hot this summer. The sun is cruel, beating upon the senses until you are dull witted and openmouthed. The air does not move. Some—like you, Nurse—become slow in the heat, caring for nothing but shade and a cool cloth to press against your sweating face. For me, the sun puts me into a trance, sets me dreaming at my window.

But it is not so for everyone. For some, sunlight sets fire to their smoldering tempers. Turns peevishness to passion. Bad humor to murderous rage. Already this summer, members of our house have twice brawled with men of the house of Montague. Yet some felt the thirst for still more blood.

That morning, I saw two men from our house, Sampson and Gregory, go out into the streets. Gregory is pleasant, but Sampson is one of those people who will tell anyone who listens what a great fighter he is—even if only he believes it.

They were not yet on the street, but Sampson was boasting that if he saw anyone of the house of Montague he would draw his sword. He said he was quick to strike, when moved. Gregory, the more mild and sensible of them, tried to tease Sampson out of his violent mood, saying as far as he had seen, Sampson was not quickly moved to do anything. I laughed at the joke because it's true, Sampson is lazy.

But jokes only seemed to spur Sampson on to darker threats. Not only would he attack any man of Montague's house, he would attack the women as well.

"Women are weak," he said. "I shall thrust them against the wall." He made a gesture with his hips.

Looking around in case someone had overheard this obnoxious remark, Gregory reminded him that the quarrel was between the masters and men. But Sampson did not care.

Listening to him, I felt a stab of fear, as if this feud had grown so hot, it would soon run out of control and we would all be consumed by it, man, woman, and child.

But then, Nurse, you came in and asked what I would wear to the feast that night and I forgot all about Gregory and Sampson.

Mother, Father, you think I do not know the world. What happens in the streets. You think I do not hear the shouting, the oaths. You think I do not see the blood upon the stones. But I do. And when I heard the shouting later that morning, I knew another brawl was upon us.

I was in my room, trying to choose a gown when I heard you, Father, shouting for a sword. Going out onto my balcony, I saw you run out to the garden in your dressing gown. Mother, you followed him, saying that a crutch would serve him better than a sword.

Both of you rushed out onto the square near our house, and disappeared from sight. More shouting, more swords clashing. People running from all corners to join the fight. Who knows what might have happened had the prince not come and put a stop to it?

Fearful, I waited by the door for you to return. A servant who had been in the square when the prince arrived told me that he was so enraged, he promised death to anyone who broke the peace again.

"Who began the quarrel?" I asked.

As I had thought, Sampson had yapped his way into a fight with two other men from the house of Montague. It was barely under way when Benvolio, a gentle youth related to the Montagues, had tried to stop it. But then Tybalt came. . . .

Tybalt, Tybalt. When I was little, I adored my darkly handsome cousin. I can remember us in the garden: Tybalt, a gallant six-year-old, striding forth to strike at the roses with a reed sword as I toddled after him. Later he snapped a bud off a rosebush and presented it to me with a bow. I still have that flower pressed in a book.

When I grew older and Nurse's powers of invention failed to conjure my fantasy prince to my satisfaction, I imagined him as Tybalt. Charming and elegant, ever gallant with ladies; Nurse, no gentleman made you blush like Tybalt did, do you remember?

I loved him so much that it was hard to believe the other stories I heard. People said that no one hated the Montagues as ferociously as Tybalt. That his hatred was almost too great. That he practiced daily with his sword, and when he was finished, he drove the blade into the target and cried, "Death to Montague!"

This summer, even I noticed a change in him. It seemed Tybalt talked of nothing but wrongs and righteousness. And he was not content to hate alone; everyone must hate and fight with him. Or we would become his enemies, too. Once I innocently ventured that there must be some honorable Montagues. He turned on me and hissed, "To think well of Montague is a betrayal of your own family." Shocked by his anger, I began to cry. He was immediately contrite and begged my pardon.

So I was not surprised to hear that Tybalt had been at the fight.

"Where are my parents?" I asked the servant. "Why aren't they home?"

He told me that the prince had demanded your presence. Child that I was, I worried the prince would keep you at his palace and our feast would be postponed.

How strange the ways of fate. If you had not been called to the prince's palace, you might not have encountered his kinsman, Count Paris. And this story might not be as sad as it is.

That afternoon, Mother, as I looked from one gown to the next and wondered if I should choose the third, you came to my chamber. At first, I thought you wanted to instruct me on how I should behave that night. For this was the first time I was allowed to attend the whole feast, from dancing to banquet. As you sat me on the bed, I expected reminders that I should not dance too long with any one gentleman, that I should keep my conversation brief and modest, and that I should remember in all things, I was a daughter of Capulet.

Instead you asked, "Juliet, what do you think of marriage?"

At first the word barely made sense. Marriage? I was only thirteen. Father had always said he did not wish me married too young. He said those married young are often unhappy.

I did not know what to say, so I replied, "I do not think about marriage." Which was true. I dreamed of love, my handsome prince coming from a faraway land—but not marriage.

Impatient, you said, "Well, start thinking about it. Because the valiant Paris, kinsman to the prince himself, loves you and wishes to marry you."

Nurse, as always, you had something to say. Paris was so good looking, you exclaimed, the very model of a man. Mother, you also gave him lavish praise. I sat there and repeated your words in my head.

Marriage. Count Paris wanted to marry me.

Because he loved me. A man I had never even seen.

I thought of him and I thought of love and I felt . . . empty.

Mother, you told me Paris would be at the feast that night. I should look at him for myself. He was handsome, you assured me of that. There was an urgency in your voice, a nervousness. I could feel that this was important to you, and I could guess why. Through this marriage, our family would be connected to the prince—something you wanted badly. You had only one child, and so only one chance to advance our family through marriage. No wonder you jumped at the opportunity.

But I couldn't do the same. For some reason, I felt stubborn. Why, I wondered, bother to ask what I wanted? What did it matter? Clearly, I was to be married to the count. It had been decided before I even had my first dance.

This is how it is for all girls, I know. I can't explain why I felt so disappointed. I thought, I would like to have been wooed by at least one other gentleman before you chose one for me, Mother.

You pressed me, telling me to answer quickly: Could I like the count?

I told you I would look at the count and hope that I liked what I saw. Then I murmured that one look wouldn't tell me much about him.

But you did not hear me. As far as you were concerned, the matter was settled.

I have loved the feast since I was a little girl, even though I was only allowed to watch from the balcony before being put to bed. Sometimes, I would creep downstairs and hide behind the tapestries, watching everyone and everything. I would gaze at the ladies, imagining myself one of them. One day, I would dance and talk and be admired in the candle-light.

Now, it seemed, there would be none of that. Flirtation, romance—I would skip it all on my way to the altar. As I dressed for the feast that night, I searched my heart and found it quiet. All the excitement I had felt earlier in the day was gone.

When I was little, I overheard Nurse say about me, "He that gets her shall have the chinks." I did not understand and so I asked her what "the chinks" meant. She turned red and said, "Oh, only the fairest, sweetest maid in all Verona." I smiled. But I knew she was lying.

When I was alone at my window, I thought about it. To get me meant getting . . . something a man might want more than me. Or as much? Perhaps I could not be loved or wanted for myself. Perhaps it was only these chinks that mattered.

"Oh," I imagined people saying, *"if you must have her, you can at least have the chinks as well."*

Then when I was a little older, I learned what chinks meant: money. My father's money. Then I imagined people saying, *"She may be small and not at all pretty or witty, but you shall get her father's money."*

As Nurse fixed my hair with special care in the early evening, I wondered, Does Paris want me or does he want the chinks? Remembering the hunger in my mother's voice, I suspected *I* was not the heart of his desire.

But then I rallied. I must not give way to gloom so easily. Perhaps Paris was exactly the prince Nurse had promised all these years. Maybe he had seen me only once but fallen madly in love. These things were possible. So perhaps I would see him once and fall madly in love back.

I have—had?—an obedient nature. What I am told to do, I often do. And this night, we were having a feast. And what should one do at a feast? Dance. Be happy. And so, I thought, whirling around the room, I shall dance and be happy!

I love night, its silence and shadows. When I was a little girl, peeking at the feast in hiding, I thought that all the most important things in life must happen at night, as if everything that truly matters must be hidden somehow. True feelings cannot belong to the workaday world of people trudging here and there, chatting of meals and weather and horses and roads. When it is dark and no one is watching, that is when we speak what we truly feel. Do what we wish to. Be who we are.

The hall was wonderful that evening. Torches flared, making every lady beautiful, every gentleman elegant. Scarlet and gold tapestries hung on the walls. The tables were full, the wine flowing. Laughter jousted with music. My dress was dark green, threaded with gold. In my hair, a crown of pearls. "Dark and light," you said, Nurse. "Your black hair, your fair skin. Pure enough to turn impure thoughts to honorable intentions." Mother, you told her to hush.

Moving carefully down the stairs, I felt like a full-grown lady. Then I realized, only a child would feel that way.

But, child that I was, I was happy. It was too wonderful to be at such a gathering. My friends and cousins and I exclaimed over our new finery and brashly speculated over which young man might fall in love with us that night.

"You shall have him," we told one another as we pointed. "And you . . . him. He? Oh, he is for you, certainly!" Girlish foolishness. We meant none of it, but enjoyed it all thoroughly.

Off to one side, not joining our game, sat my cousin Rosaline. Rosaline was from my mother's side of the family, and she had my mother's look. A little older than I, Rosaline held herself at a distance, so it was easy to think of her as a rare and fine creature. She had a dark, icy beauty. Her raven hair fell just so over her exquisite face. Her nose was long and elegant, her eye scornful. I confess, I did not always like her, yet I always yearned for her good opinion.

"And who is for Rosaline?" I asked.

"God alone," said one cousin, rolling her eyes. "She has sworn she will stay chaste and never marry."

"Ah, no," said another mischievous girl. "That is only what she tells that poor boy who is so in love with her, so that he will leave her alone."

"What boy is that?" I asked, wide-eyed.

Each looked to the other. No one, it seemed, knew his name. "But he is mad for her," said the gossip. "They say his heart and mind are nearly broken with love. He spends his days sighing and weeping because she is so cold. His family is quite worried," she added with a wicked little smile.

"Poor boy—why does Rosaline scorn him?" I asked.

"Because she is an ice maid," said my cousin, bored with the subject.

And though our talk turned to other things, my mind stayed on that sad young man who loved Rosaline. I wished someone loved me like that. But I would never have the heart to torment a boy who loved me so deeply. If someone loved me truly, I would—

Then a group of young men romped into the hall. They all wore masks, so it was impossible to know who they were. But since they were disguised, it was easy to guess they hadn't been invited. It was the custom for adventurous young men to come uninvited, it added excitement. Besides, they were handsomely dressed and carried themselves with grace. Immediately, a whispering went up among my little band. *Who are they?* We had great fun guessing: Who was that one? Who this one?

Looking around me, I thought happily, anyone might be anybody and anything might happen. And then I remembered, there was no mystery about my fate. I would marry Paris. I felt that dullness in my heart again.

We were not the only ones to notice the boys' arrival. My cousin Tybalt turned storm-faced and went directly to you, my father. Like me, you loved a festival. You were always welcoming everyone, making sure everybody had enough to eat and drink and that the music kept all spirits light.

So no wonder you looked annoyed when Tybalt approached. I did not hear all your words, but I knew Tybalt's mood had something to do with the new arrivals. Doubtless, he was angry that these young men were here without permission. I heard him shout that these were villains, and he would not endure them. But you, Father, being more open-hearted, refused to throw them out.

Now, I wonder, had you known what would happen, would you have done as Tybalt asked?

I did as you told me, my parents, and looked for Paris. I hoped to find him handsome and kind. I told myself I should be happy. I was about to see the man I would marry. I was about to begin my life as a woman. Yet when I thought of Paris, it seemed like my life was ending.

I confess that I did not look as hard as I could have. But shortly after Tybalt's tantrum, I heard a voice greet me by name. I turned to see a tall, richly dressed man. My eyes, rather than my heart, saw that he was handsome. He gave me his name and asked me to dance.

This was Paris. I said yes.

We shared a careful dance, the count and I. We talked of . . . I do not remember the details. Hawking. The weather. He found ways to tell me he had many fine connections. The prince was mentioned several times. As was his cousin, Mercutio.

"Have you met Mercutio?" he asked.

I said I had not—at least I did not think so.

"Oh, you would remember Mercutio, if you had met him,"

the count assured me. "A fiery, poetic gentleman. Often caught up in fantasy. But one is never bored in his company." I would like to dance with Mercutio, I thought, rather than the one who holds my hand now—and forever, if he and my parents have their way.

As we danced, I thought, This is my future, walking side by side with this man. I tried to find my fantasy prince in him. This version of my prince was gold haired with hazel eyes, one of the few combinations Nurse and I had not imagined. Certainly, he was wealthy. Certainly, noble. And he said he loved me, although I did not feel it. Because if he loved me, shouldn't I feel happier in his company? Shouldn't I feel freer to share my thoughts with someone who supposedly wished to have my heart? Why was I so stingy in my replies and in my looks?

Mother, I could feel you watching us from across the room. It did not put me at ease.

The dance ended. I curtsied. When I looked up into Paris' smiling face, I did not care if I never saw it again.

I was not sure where to go next. Tybalt stalked back and forth near the fire, keeping his eyes upon the masked newcomers. He had always had time for me before, but he would not be interested in my girlish business now. Mother, you stood in one part of the hall, awaiting reports. In another, my female cousins, also wanting news. Nurse, you fluttered here and there, searching for me.

I looked for you, Father, and found you standing near Paris. You beckoned me over. And I realized, Yes, it is Father who has what Paris wants. The richness of the feast, the fineness of our house. In a rare moment of defiance, I thought,

Yes, he shall have the chinks. But he shall not have me.

Perhaps that is why, rather than coming when you called, I did a very childish thing and hid. Gathering my skirts, I ducked in between dancers and servers and onlookers and slipped behind one of the curtains.

It was the same as when I was younger, peeking out to watch the grown-ups. But as much as I had wanted to join the festivities then, I was glad to be away from them now. I played the old game. If I could choose, what man would I have for my own?

I saw things differently than I had when I was a child— or even a few hours ago. Now, I looked past the beautiful eyes and fine clothes and saw things I did not like. So many men's faces were closed. Their eyes hard. From this distance, away from the dance, I noticed that it was the older married men who paid the most attention to the ladies, paying them compliments or whirling them around the dance floor. The younger ones seemed restless and angry like my cousin Tybalt. The simple joys of life seemed to bore them.

None, I thought. I would choose none that I see here.

I laid my hand on the stone pillar, cool in the heat of the crowd and the flames of the fire. I thought of churches and cemeteries. This might be the last feast I attended as a maid. From here, I would go to church and be married. After that, I would be a mother to children—until they were married off as I was about to be. I would grow old, stout, and gray haired. I would complain of my aches like the nurse. And then, off to my grave.

Was that a life? Everything I had dreamed, would it really amount to so little?

My parents, as I think of how to tell you what happened next, I am almost afraid. But perhaps since I am dead, it is better that you hate me. Perhaps it will make it easier for you to be without me. I will tell myself I am being kind in telling you the truth. I pray that I am.

I felt a hand over mine. At first the fingers just touched the tips of mine; then they lay over them, warm and gentle. I did not look. I was afraid to. Our palms met. Before I even laid eyes on him, we were joined.

I turned and saw . . .

Well, how shall I say what I saw?

A boy. A youth. He wore a mask, so I knew he had come uninvited. It was bright blue and winged, like a bird. A lock of dark hair fell across it. His eyes were large and dark. They searched mine, looking for . . . what? I was not sure, but I was aware of a desperate desire that they might find what they sought, whether it was beauty or an answer or . . . *Yes,* I found myself thinking, hoping it showed in my eyes. *Yes, yes.*

He was slender, but the hand over mine was strong. His mouth was full, parted slightly in hope.

Oh, if he is looking for someone else, I thought, I will die.

Our hands were already touching. His fingers moved slightly. I parted mine without thinking, and our fingers threaded together. He smiled and so did I. No, he was not looking for someone else.

He made a little game, pretending he was a pilgrim and I was a saint's statue.

He said, "If I've offended by touching with my unworthy

hands, I will soothe the hurt by kissing the spot my hand has soiled."

Despite my happiness, I was slightly shocked that he would talk of kissing so soon. And besides, I must be true to the game. Would a saint accept such boldness?

Taking my hand back from him, I said, "Pilgrims' hands are best used in prayer," and put my palms together to show him.

"Do saints have lips?" he asked.

"Of course," I said. "But like hands, they are best used in prayer."

I stepped back around the pillar, but he followed, as if we were two children around a maypole.

"If lips and hands are so alike," he wondered, "might not lips meet as hands do, pressed together?"

It took me a moment to understand his meaning. Our hands had touched; why not our lips? I knew that most of my female cousins would have stopped the game here. And so should I.

But I, entranced, thought of those saints' statues I prayed to. After all, if someone wished to kiss a statue, what could it do?

I whispered, "Saints do not move, but grant favors asked in prayer."

"Then move not," he said, "as I pray."

As we kissed, I was aware of the cold stone at my back, my palms and fingers flat against the marble. I felt his life's warmth and weight press against me. I did not want to stop, and gave him many little after-kisses, like a bird wanting more from another's mouth.

I murmured that now his sin was on my lips, and he swore he would take it back again. And so he did, until our mouths were open and my hands were no longer pressed against the stone, but twined in his hair.

Nurse, I suppose we were lucky it was you who came upon us. And that when you did, we were no longer so tangled. Still, I think your sharp eyes caught something, because you said my mother wanted me in a voice much louder than necessary.

I swear, I had forgotten I had parents. Or that anyone existed in the world, save for the young man in the blue mask.

Who I had just kissed. Without even knowing his name. I, who was about to be engaged to another man. In a burst of confusion, I hurried back to the festivities in search of my mother.

Mother, I dimly recall giving half answers to your whispered questions. I had danced with the count? What did he say? Did I like him? Yes, we had danced, I said, he said . . . I don't remember.

You pressed. "Did you like him?"

"Well, I . . ."

I felt certain that the burning blush of what had happened was clear for all to see. Surely my lips were bruised, my hair loose, my eyes wild. My fingers felt at my neck, my thigh, brushed my breast. I could think of nothing but that young man.

Only a little while later, I saw him again. He and his friends were leaving. Father—sweet Father!—you invited them to stay longer, but they would not. Why, I wondered, does he not look for me as I look for him? Perhaps he has kissed me—and who knows who else at the feast—and now leaves in search of another party and other ladies? No. It cannot have meant so little to him and so much to me!

Nurse, I asked you what his name was, so that I might at least be able to investigate and learn his reputation. To mask my interest, I asked about several men; infuriatingly, my young man in the blue mask was the only one you did not know. So I sent you to find out. At the time, my greatest fear was that he was not free. If he is married, I thought, my grave will be my wedding bed.

Alas, you returned with worse news. Not married, but Montague.

"Romeo," you said, breathless with surprise that he would dare come to our house. "The only son of your great enemy."

As I watched him slip away, I recalled a day when I was small, not yet six. I was playing in the garden, following a ball that had rolled too far, when men came. They carried another man. He was blanched white and seemed to sleep. His shirt was wet and dark with blood, so drenched it clung to his ribs. But at his side, I saw that his flesh was open, a great gaping hole.

I had not known flesh was so heavy, so engorged with blood. It was not something I should look on, I knew, but I could not look away. I had the strange desire to touch the wound, to understand his flesh with my fingers, as if bodies might speak to each other.

Mother, you screamed. Nurse, you clapped a hand over my eyes and hurried me away. I cried, and you thought I was frightened. But I was sorry to be taken away; I wanted to stay with that man, to know what life and death felt like.

That night is the first I can remember hearing the name of Montague. Over and over in a rush of curses and threats. I began to understand that Montague was somehow part of the blood and the flesh. Montague had brought a strange madness to our house, making my mother cry and my father shout until I worried the very walls would fall.

Montague had slain our kinsman! Montague had broken the peace! Montague the cruel! Murderous Montague!

Nurse, I asked questions. But for once, you were short with me, saying, No more talk. Quiet now.

But there was more, much more. When I was older, there were toasts at family gatherings. Death to Montague! With your arm around my shoulder, Father, I raised my cup and cried, Death to Montague! You laughed and kissed me.

What, to me, was Montague? For whom did I wish death? In my mind, Montague was an old man, a brawl in the streets, all the ugly, bloody, sharp-edged things that lay beyond my walls. Back then it seemed harmless to say "Death to Montague!"

Now as I looked to the place Romeo had stood, I recalled all this and thought: But oh, my sweet, sweet love, you are Montague. Your dear face, your lovely voice—why did no one tell me? This, too, is Montague. Not just hatred and feuding and danger. But love and sweetness and holding and, oh, everything!

Pleading tiredness, I practically ran to my room. My mind was in a storm. I had begun this day as a child, fretting over which dress to wear. By midday, I was, for all intents and purposes, engaged. By evening, I had met the man I was to marry and decided I did not like him and that my life was over. Not an hour after that, I met the only man I would ever love, but he was a sworn enemy to my family. What game was fate playing with me?

And I had kissed him. Our lips had met not once but twice. I had always thought myself modest. I had no reason not to. Until now, men I did not know made me wordlessly shy. Then who could this Juliet be who opened her mouth and pressed her body against a man scant minutes after she laid eyes on him?

It was then that I remembered an old story Nurse liked to tell. In truth, she repeated it so often, I barely listened anymore. I had been a baby, unskilled at walking, when I fell forward and hurt my head. Nurse's husband was a big merry man given to laughing. He lifted me up and made a joke that when I was older, I would know better and fall backward. Since I was just a baby, I said, Aye.

For years, I did not understand why that made people laugh. Then something in the laughter told me it pertained to the bedchamber. Girls who fell backward usually found boys on top of them. To those adult ears, my childish "aye" had sounded wanton, as if I were eager for such a tumble.

Maybe my "aye" was prophecy. Perhaps my infant self had known my elder self better than anyone supposed. I hardly knew myself. Kissing a man—and a Montague!—in such a way, I was neither chaste nor worthy of the name Capulet. I had changed so much since the morning.

After the feast, I wandered restlessly in my room. Every doubt, every horror entered my head: *How could I kiss a Montague? I must never see him again.* And yet every no led back to its opposite. *How could I not kiss him? How could I not love him? I must.* I nearly went mad with the snarl of thought and feeling.

The night was still and close. There seemed to be no air in my room. Choked with emotion, I could not breathe. And so I went out onto the balcony where the darkness gave me a little freedom. The stone was cool and friendly under my hands. Summer roses, gray-pink in the moonlight, gave the air a sweet scent. Somewhere, a nightingale sang.

Alone in the dark, with no one to hear but the wind and the trees, I quickly forgot those *how coulds* and *must nevers*. Those words belonged to others, I realized. My parents, the old Montagues. Tybalt. In my own mind, one question took hold. "How," I wondered aloud, "could I be with Romeo?"

Trying to be practical for a moment, I reasoned. Several things stood in our way. The first, his name. He was a Montague. Well, I thought, and what of it? Montague was not evil incarnate—no matter what my cousin Tybalt might say. Who were the Montagues? Yes, they were Romeo's father and Romeo's kin, and some of these people were enemies of our house. But . . . Romeo's grandmother, Romeo's infant cousins, if he had any. They could not be called "enemies." And neither could Romeo. Surely if he were an enemy, he would never have started our little game of saints and pilgrims.

Oh, but . . . he might not have known who I was then. But he would be sure to find out. And when he found out, would he still love me? My face, my voice, my true self would be the same as he saw at the feast. Once he learned all these bore the name of Capulet, it would not change his feelings, would it?

And by the same token, I could not let his name of Montague change my feelings for him. Looking at the roses, I thought you could call them delphinium or snapdragon or . . . skunkweed. But an ugly name would not change the beauty of their perfume.

In fact, the more I thought about it, the giddier I grew. Unlike Paris—who I was now convinced only loved me for my name and fortune—Romeo loved me in spite of who my father was.

But could his family? Another difficulty presented itself. His family would almost certainly refuse me. And if they did? Would Romeo choose me or his name?

Faced with the choice between being loved by Romeo and being a Capulet, I knew which I would pick, and shouted as much to the night. "Romeo," I cried, "give up your name. Or if you won't—and you love me—I'll no longer be a Capulet."

You can imagine my shock when the night answered. Bounding into a silver-gray patch of moonlight, Romeo shouted, "Love me and I'll nevermore be Romeo!"

In the shadow and moonlight, it was difficult at first to see who stood below my balcony. I thought it some trick, a drunken guest making jests. But when Romeo spoke a little more, I was sure it was him.

And I was terrified. Remembering Tybalt's black mood, I knew that a Montague taking such liberties as to stand under my balcony, with me in my dressing gown, would be all the excuse he needed for bloodshed.

As much as I loved the sight of Romeo, I begged him to

go, warning him that my kinsmen would kill him if they found him there.

He said that my look was far more dangerous to him than any sword. That if I but looked sweetly upon him, he could do battle with twenty kinsmen.

When one you love speaks so lovingly, it is wonderful to hear. Still, I must be sure we were—and would stay—alone.

"You haven't told anyone you were coming here?" I asked. "No one gave you directions or helped you over the orchard walls?" Because I could imagine a Sampson or Gregory gossiping—and that gossip quickly reaching the wrong ears.

"No!" he shouted. "Love showed me the way. Love helped me leap over the walls."

He was so sure and happy—so fearless!—that my fears faded. Perhaps I should have been more like my cousin Rosaline: cold and distant. Or played a masterful game of coyness and flirtation. But we had already gone too far for pouts and half promises; he knew I was no champion at that game.

And so I asked him bluntly, "Do you love me?"

How did I find the courage to be so straight? Because in my heart, I knew his answer was yes.

Yet even as I asked, I realized how little I knew about the rules of love. Perhaps Romeo would think I was being too forward. I really should be more ladylike.

But I felt I could tell him anything, and so I said, "I know you'll say yes, you love me. And whatever you say, I'll believe you. So please be honest. Or if you think I'm too bold, if you want me to pretend and frown and say I don't care, I will." Here I leaned farther over the balcony. "But I do love you. More truly than those ladies who can say no over and over again." Here I was thinking of my cousin Rosaline. "And it's foolish to act as if I don't love you when you've already heard me say so when I thought no one was listening."

Romeo stopped my babbling and swore by the moon, "I do love you."

I replied, "Do not swear by the changeable moon, which is sometimes full, sometimes a sliver. That would mean one day you love me and the next you barely remember I exist."

"What should I swear by, then?" he asked, grinning.

"Swear on yourself," I told him. "For you are my god."

Which was far too bold, and I scolded myself. This was too much and too soon. I would wear out his love with words. And so I tried to say good night and withdraw.

He cried out, "How can you leave me so unsatisfied?"

Which stopped me. What, exactly, did he mean? Fearful, hopeful, I turned. "What satisfaction can you have tonight?"

And so I was drawn back into the night again and we talked until you, Nurse, called me in. At this, I remembered that other world of families—Montague and Capulet, daytime brawls, and Tybalt's angry looks. With that, came doubt. How could we overcome all this? It was easy to say pretty things about the power of love, but when daylight and reality returned . . . where would our love stand then? Pretending I had left something on the balcony, I raced outside again.

"A few words, Romeo, and then good night," I whispered. "If you love me—"

He opened his mouth, prepared to swear again that he did. I interrupted, saying, "And want to marry me?"

I watched his face for signs of hesitation. To my joy, I saw none. "I shall send my nurse to you tomorrow. Tell her where and when I should meet you and I'll lay my fortunes at your feet and follow you throughout the world."

Called inside again, I hurried, "But if this has been just a lover's game? Then stop it at once. Because it's not a game to me."

Only when I was back inside did I realize I did not know what time to send the nurse. And so, another forgotten item to be retrieved! I ran back outside and called down to Romeo, "Love, what time shall I send the nurse?" I prayed he did not make me wait all day.

"At nine in the morning," he said.

"I shall not fail," I told him. "It will seem like twenty years till then."

Then I just stood gazing down at him. It seemed there must be more to say, a way to prolong this wondrous night.

I said, "I have forgotten now why I called you back."

"I'll wait," said Romeo, "until you remember."

"I wish you were a bird. Then I could keep you on a silken string and tug you back when you flew too far away from me." He smiled.

I knew as morning approached, it grew more and more dangerous for him to be here. But I could not bear to let him go. "Parting is sweet sorrow. Perhaps I could say good night until tomorrow . . ."

Finally, I could think of nothing more and went back inside my house. It was torment to do so. There were hours yet between now and nine. Romeo would have too much time to think and think again. Perhaps this love was just a night's fantasy. Or if not, would he truly give up his name and his family for me?

For myself, I already knew.

Oh, I can hear you now, my parents: *"Stupid, naive child—all he had to do was speak a few honey words to her and she fancied herself in love." "And"*—Mother, I think you will add this part—*"does she not know that it's this same Romeo who was so lovesick for Rosaline? Here is a boy who loves deeply indeed! Why, that very night he had come to our feast hoping to woo her cousin!"*

Yes, I know all that. I know because he told me. We all have our fancies before we meet the one we truly love; have I not admitted my own silly dreams about Tybalt? In Rosaline, Romeo loved only her beauty—which, I admit, is powerful. But he did not love her heart, for she has none.

Do not scold Romeo for a fickle heart, my parents. Don't you see fate at work when two fools go looking for others and find each other instead? Nurse, as you say, fate has a way of catching those blind enough to think they control their future.

And you will see, his love for me proved true enough later on.

I do not think I slept that night. Nurse, I can remember hearing you snore beyond my bed-curtains and thinking not even such an ugly noise could distract me from my lovely thoughts of Romeo.

And yet I must have slept, for I awoke at daybreak, full of fire and purpose. Immediately I roused you. Dragging you from your bed, I said I had an errand for you. Dress! And hurry! (It was just past six when I did, and I confess, this really was too early. But it seemed the sooner the day's business was begun, the sooner would I know if Romeo wanted me for wife or not.)

Oh, what complaint there was, until I whispered my secret to you. You were to play Cupid for me. You clapped your hands, thinking I meant Paris. You were all eagerness to help—until I said no, it was not Paris. It was Romeo, son of Montague.

Good nurse, I think you did love me, truly. You fretted when I told you who my love was, but then you set aside those fears and jumped in with me. You could have told my parents, might have shouted at me, dragged me to church for prayers and repentance. But you didn't. No matter what betrayals came after, I shall always remember that.

You used to call me a wise and patient child. Well, I was no wise and patient child that morning. I sent you out at a little before nine, then spent what seemed eternity waiting for you to return. I am ashamed to admit that I blamed you, cursing your age, your lameness and slowness. Old people, I thought, know nothing about love; they have forgotten what it feels like, if indeed they ever felt it at all. If you could understand the love I felt, I reasoned brokenly, you would be that much faster to give me my news.

When I could not fill my mind by railing against you, I worried about other things. Romeo would not come. He would come, but you would not find each other. You would find each other, but his news would be sad. He had only trifled with me. There would be an idle apology. "Go, tell your mistress I am heartily sorry she did mistake my poetic mood for love. . . ."

But whatever ugly things I thought about you that morning, I was much punished when you finally did come back. It took me forever to get the news from you.

When you came through the door, I leaped up, crying, "Good sweet nurse!" Then I saw your face and asked, "Why do you look so sad? If it's bad news, you should make it sound better by telling me in a happy voice. And if it's good news, don't look so sour!"

"I'm weary!" you moaned. "Let me rest. My bones ache."

Well, I wished I had your bones and your news. I begged you to tell me what Romeo had said.

"Wait a moment," you said. "I can't speak; I'm out of breath."

"How can you have no breath to speak when you have enough breath to tell me you can't speak?" I demanded. "Is your news good or bad? Tell me that and I'll let you rest."

At this point, you vexed me further by telling me foolish nothings I already knew of Romeo, how handsome he was, how gentle, and so on. "I know all this," I told you. "What did he say about marriage?" By this time, I was pleading.

"Oh, my head hurts," you said. "It feels like it's about to break into pieces. And my back! It aches so. Shame on you for sending me on such a rough journey. All this running around will be the death of me!"

I began to worry you would be lost in sulks, and I would never get my news. And so I soothed and rubbed and spoke sweetly, saying, "I am sorry you are not well. Sweet, sweet,

sweet nurse, please. Please tell me? What says my love?"

You leaned in and whispered, "Your love says—where's your mother?"

I started. "Inside. What do you mean, where's my mother? What does my mother have to do with it?"

More moans. "Is this the thanks I get for my pains? From now on, you can get your messages yourself."

"What a fuss!" I said. "Tell me, what did Romeo say?"

Then at last—at last!—you told me, "Get yourself to Friar Laurence's, Juliet, and there be married Romeo."

No doubt many have rushed to church before when they were in sore need of confession and forgiveness. I, who had only two kisses (but many thoughts) to count among my sins, hurried to the chapel like a desperate penitent. People on the street probably wondered at my haste. Keeping my smiles down, I thought, "I am getting married today! And no one, save the nurse, knows!"

Had any girl rushed to marriage with such joy as I? I couldn't imagine so. No matter how fast I went, it was not fast enough to outrun worry. What if Romeo was delayed? Or decided not to come? Could such happiness actually be mine and so fast? Just yesterday, when my mother broke the news of Paris' hopes, I thought myself doomed to a dull and dutiful match. And now . . . when I thought of what I went to, I ran even faster than before.

All my fears proved foolish. Romeo was waiting within the chapel, looking as eager and worried as me. When we met, we kissed so much that the good friar swore we should not be left alone till we were wed. In faith, I think he was right.

It is funny how few words it takes to get married, to turn two people into one. And yet, maybe it's not so odd because when two are already one in spirit, as Romeo and I were, how many words do you really need?

(Mother, Father, you must not be angry with the friar for marrying us. He did it from true Christian desire to see the feud between our houses ended. He sought only to prevent more blood being shed. Indeed, I do not see how anyone could look at the friar's balding head, his round belly, his kind, gray eyes and see anything but charity. I beg you, save your rage for me alone. It was not his fault.)

Once married, I could not stand to see my new husband go, wanting to hold him as tightly as his ring now clasped my finger. I kept my arm around his neck, kissing his cheek, his mouth, his shoulder. I was suddenly possessed by the fear that if I let him go for a little while, I might have to let him go forever. Romeo laughed and called me fanciful. What could go wrong? We were married now. What could happen that would part us? All that was left now was for him to tell his parents that the Capulet–Montague feud was now at an end. If they objected, well, it was too bad. We were married. Marriage had not changed our natures. Romeo was still ever hopeful, while I was given to doubts and fears.

But Romeo had reassured me and so I let him go. He promised to come to me that night. I did not think I would be able to wait the hours. That afternoon was one of the longest I have ever known.

And yet, I might have wished our story ended there. That I never let Romeo go and we stayed together always. For when Romeo and I went our separate ways, misery followed close behind.

As I went home, a new married bride, I wanted to run, leap, and whirl about until the motion of my body matched the wild happiness in my heart.

There is a dance for love; also a dance for death. When you mean to kill someone, you are at first most polite. A letter is sent, an entreaty made. Meet me at such and such a place. The forms are followed. It shall be this weapon; you shall bring these supporters. The two parties meet. And someone is killed.

Tybalt sent Romeo such a letter the morning after the feast.

It is hard for me not to take some of the blame in this matter. Did Tybalt know, I wonder, about me and Romeo? Did he spy on us from the other side of the curtain? Did he overhear me ask who the masked gentleman was and gasp when I learned the truth?

No, actually, I do not think it was our love that sent Tybalt into that fight. That fight was destined long before I saw Romeo. If it was our fate to love each other, it was Tybalt's fate to kill. . . .

And to be killed.

All that day, unable to think about anything except Romeo, I claimed to be sick so that I would not be bothered. I lay on my bed and thought of how he would come to me that night and what was to happen. Tonight, we would not stop at kissing. No more silly games of saints and prayers. I would see all of him, touch all of him. And he would see and touch all of me. Time seemed so dull, existence so pointless until then!

The stubborn sun hung fixed in the sky. It seemed the light would never dim, the cheerful chatter of day never give way to night. A minute was an hour, an hour a day, a day a lifetime.

I wondered about other wedding nights, when two near-strangers meet as man and wife, naked, until robed in each other's bodies. Nurse, when you first told me of what goes on between men and women, I laughed, thinking it one of your country stories. "Surely, my parents never did such things!" Well, I was a child.

Heat lulls the mind and stirs the body. It quiets the voices that hiss, "Immodest! Sinful!" It was no sin to want my husband, I told myself. But if he had not been my husband, I would have wanted him just the same. I rolled over on my side, shut my eyes, and tried to sleep. This was worse. To shut my eyes allowed other, wilder visions that made me even more restless.

How many hours passed in this way? One? Three? I was not sure whether I slept or not. But I came out of my drowsy, love-drugged state to the sound of screaming in the court-yard. Very like, I thought dimly, the screaming that I heard when I was but six years old. . . .

I hate to think on this.

Nurse, you came to my rooms. Usually, you were slow in making your way. But this time, you hurried, as if trying to escape some frightful thing.

In your hand, you carried the ropes for the ladder that would bring Romeo to me that night. In your agitation, you twisted and twisted it, until it was tight around your arms and the blood turned dark in your fingers.

Frightened, I asked, "What's happened?"

And you burst out with the awful words, "He's dead, he's dead, he's dead."

My mind was so fixed on Romeo, I felt sure it was he who was dead, even before you began to wail his name. I joined you in weeping and begged to know, "Has he killed himself?" Because I would quickly do the same if so.

Then you said, "I saw the wound. It was on his chest. Oh, he was pitiful, pale as ashes, smeared in blood. I nearly fainted."

When you talked of wounds, I began to understand that this was no suicide. But then you began to moan Tybalt's name. And I realized, Tybalt—too?—was dead.

Was it hope? Stupidity? Why did I not realize, knowing Tybalt's rage, what had happened?

Some accident, I thought, some evil has killed both my cousin and my love on the same day. I began to cry for them both. I could not bear to think about Romeo, but every fond memory of Tybalt flooded my brain: Tybalt as a black-eyed six-year-old helping me up after I had fallen, Tybalt giving gallant compliments to my ten-year-old self at Christmas, his kindness to you, Nurse, his rosebud, dry and pressed flat in a book somewhere. What had I done that fate would take from me two of the dearest people in my life?

Then you spat the truth at me: Tybalt was dead and Romeo had killed him. Now Romeo was banished.

Romeo killed Tybalt. I repeated the words in my head, trying to get them to make sense. Romeo killed . . . no, no, that was wrong. It must be wrong. It couldn't be true!

But when I looked at your red, tearstained face, Nurse, I knew you had no reason to lie.

I was furious. How could I have been so wrong about Romeo? I had thought him so different from the rest: gentle, joyful, kind. But he had gone from our wedding to a street fight—and killed my own dear cousin. He was not kind, not gentle. He was the same as all the rest: hateful, living only to kill or die. I had been blinded by his beauty into thinking a sweet face meant a sweet temper. How could I have made such a terrible mistake?

Those who are cruel should be ugly, I thought. Nature should give us clues as to a man's true self. A twisted soul should be housed in a twisted body. Never should one who could murder his own wife's cousin be so beautiful. . . .

Then, Nurse, you said there was no honesty in men, no faith. Calling for drink, you bleated, "Shame to Romeo!"

When you cursed his name, I heard my own anger echoed back at me, and it was then I felt a different shame. How could I, Romeo's wife of a few hours, abandon him so quickly? Yes, he had murdered Tybalt, but . . .

But given the chance, Tybalt would have murdered him. This truth was so clear, I felt all my early rage seep away. It was Tybalt who had sought a fight with Romeo, not the other way around. And once Tybalt had begun a fight, it did not end until someone was in his grave. Would I want that someone to be Romeo?

No. I had been lucky and not even realized it.

But there had been something else you had said, Nurse. Some other terrible news that I was now forgetting. My mind shied away even as I tried to remember what it was.

Tybalt was dead, yes, and Romeo safe because Tybalt was dead. That was good, but there was something else. Romeo was . . .

Banished.

Forbidden to live within Verona's walls. On pain of death.

And so, in truth, Romeo was as good as dead to me.

It was then that I first thought I would die. I would hang myself with the very ropes Romeo had given me to make a ladder to my chamber. I, a maid, would die maiden-widowed, and death, not Romeo, would have my maidenhead.

So much did I trust you, Nurse, that I told you what I meant to do. You turned pale and begged me not to. You promised to go to Romeo for me, fetch him so that I might say farewell.

I thought you were so kind when you did that. But now I am not sure. Perhaps it would have been better to die then when I was full resolved in bitterness and despair.

But if I had killed myself then, I would never have had my one full night with Romeo. That was a heaven I would not give up, even if it meant losing my chance of heaven hereafter.

Some men are arrogant after killing. They brag about their cruelty. But not Romeo. Horrified by what he had done, he came to me in tears, saying, "You must think me an old murderer." I ran to him and held him there on the floor. Cradled in my arms, he said he had destroyed our happiness before we even began our lives together. Even as I murmured comfort, what he said struck me hard. He was right: How could we be happy now? He offered to kill himself. But I said that if he did that, he would kill me as well.

Clutching at his leg, then his arm, he cried, "What part of me is my name? If I could find it, I would cut it out."

I begged him not to talk of hurting himself. He said, "The friar said I must be reasonable, that the prince has been merciful. Merciful! To go into exile is the same as death." He stroked my face. "Heaven is here with you. What do priests know? If he were young like us, in love like us—he wouldn't talk about reason and mercy."

He wanted to tell me what had happened, so that I might understand. I did not want him to, for I did not want our little time together spent on something that could not be helped.

But it was important to him that I know how he came to kill Tybalt when it was the last thing in the world he meant to do. And so I let him tell me the awful story.

After we were wed, he was on his way to his father's house when he came upon his friends Mercutio and Benvolio in the square. The moment he saw them, he sensed all was not well. Their hands on their swords, each had a watchful air. A little distance away, others had gathered to see the fight they felt sure was coming.

Then Romeo saw Tybalt.

And Tybalt saw Romeo. Immediately, he ended whatever conversation he had with Mercutio, saying, "Peace be with you, here comes my man." And headed straight for Romeo.

"Romeo," he said, "you are a villain."

Romeo stopped in his story here to say he had never noticed before that Tybalt and I looked much alike. "When I looked into his eyes, I saw yours. And I couldn't be angry with him."

But Romeo's friends were crowing and catcalling, certain that after such an insult, a duel would follow. Romeo said, "Tybalt, I like you, for reasons I cannot give. So I'll ignore the insult and say only, Farewell. I see you do not know me."

This gentle answer pleased no one—least of all Tybalt. He snarled, "That does not excuse your injuries to my family. Turn and draw."

Badly provoked, Romeo stayed calm. "I never injured you, Tybalt. Indeed, I love your family more than you can imagine. I hope that puts an end to this."

But the spirit of this terrible feud could never be satisfied by such sweet reason. And this time, it was not a Capulet, but a Montague who was outraged. When Romeo tried to walk away, Mercutio, who, in his own way was as fierce as Tybalt, could not accept what he saw as a coward's flight. Tybalt's insult must be answered—by Romeo's friends if Romeo would not do it himself.

Leaping after Tybalt, he shouted, "Tybalt, you rat-catcher, will you run away?"

At first, Tybalt, so fixed on Romeo, was not interested. "What do you want with me?" he asked.

Mercutio taunted him, saying, "Good king of cats, one of your nine lives."

(I did not say so to Romeo, but I felt a flash of anger that Mercutio would threaten my cousin so. But then I remembered, it was not Mercutio who had killed Tybalt.) And so the fight began. Knowing the prince's order against street brawls, Romeo and his friend Benvolio tried to separate the pair, who were by now both enraged and slashing away at each other. Romeo was desperate that no friend of his would hurt Tybalt. Several times, he attempted to grab Mercutio's arm or shoulder.

"Maybe I was wrong," he said to me. "But a man fighting a duel will listen to nothing but the clash of steel. You have to hold him to make him stop."

And that is what he did. And that is when Tybalt struck.

Crying again, Romeo said, "I know he didn't mean to kill him. It seemed like he'd just cut him a little. The wound didn't seem that bad."

Ever the joker, Mercutio claimed it was just a scratch. But he said, "It is enough. Anyone who asks for me tomorrow shall find me a 'grave' man."

"We laughed," Romeo remembered. "My friend was dying and I laughed."

Even when Mercutio screamed, "A plague on both your houses!" everyone thought it a joke. A surgeon would be called, Romeo told himself, the wound attended to. No blood—no real blood—had been shed. He had kept the peace between the houses. We were safe, he and I. . . .

But then pale Mercutio asked Romeo, "Why? Why did you come between me and Tybalt? It was under your arm I was hurt."

Moments later, Mercutio was dead.

"I killed him," Romeo told me. "I kept hearing Mercutio calling me a coward and asking why I tried to stop the fight. Then I remembered Tybalt calling me villain, how weak I was with him. And I thought, I am a coward. I am a villain."

So when he caught sight of Tybalt—gloating over Mercutio's corpse or so it seemed to Romeo's grief-maddened senses—Romeo drew and . . .

Here I stopped him. I did not want to hear of Tybalt's slaying. I knew what had happened, I told him. He need not repeat it. But he did, in such a choked, shamed voice that even if I had wanted to blame him, I could not have. Mother, Father, I feel sure that even you would have been moved to pity if you had heard him.

No, you will say, *Never pity a Montague*. Well, who shall pity Mercutio? If it had been Romeo killed, do you think his mother would not have wept for him as you weep now for Tybalt? Remember, it was Tybalt who first sought to shed blood.

Montague. Capulet. Are these two so different? Certainly, we seem to act the same. The men threaten and brawl. They fight—and they die. Meanwhile the women wail and pray. And the men who are left vow revenge. And so it begins again.

There was nothing for me to say to my poor boy. So I only held him and gave him what comfort I could without words.

What was it that woke me the next morning? A pierce of light through the curtain? Birdsong? No, I think it was a chill, a sense that I was losing something, and I must wake up and get it back.

When I opened my eyes, I saw Romeo standing by the bed, trying to put on his clothes as quietly as he could so as not to wake me. The thought that he might have left me sleeping panicked me and I snatched at his shirt, saying there was no need to leave. It was not yet day. The bird that sang was a nightingale, no shrill lark of morning. There was still time; he did not have to go.

He looked sad, so unlike the boy who had stood below my balcony, proclaiming he could leap over its walls if I gave him one word of love. I thought, Why, he is old. What has happened to him? Who has stolen his joy and hope?

Then I realized, I was his wife. I must be his joy and hope. I must make light of our woes and help him believe everything was still possible. So I insisted that no, no, it was not day at all. He was mistaken. Why, it was obviously night! The light we saw was not the dawn, but a . . . meteor! A meteor streaking across the sky to light his way to Mantua. So, I said, hugging him and pulling him back down onto the bed, he must not leave me yet.

He laughed—whether from genuine mirth or to console me, I do not know—and played along. Certainly, it was not yet morning, he said. He would stay, stay and be put to death if I willed it so.

His talk of death chilled me. I had forgotten the penalty for trespass after banishment was death. If Romeo was discovered in Verona, the prince would execute him. This game had dire consequences. And in any case, we were not children; we were past games now.

Pulling the sheet over my breasts, I told him to go. It was the lark, not the nightingale. He must leave, and quickly, because I was on the verge of sobbing and knew my tenderhearted love would never go if he saw me in tears.

Then there was a knock at the door. A whispered voice—yours, Nurse—warned us that Mother was on her way to my chamber. Romeo leaped up and gathered the rest of his things. Pulling a robe about me, I hurried with him to the balcony. The morning was gray, the sun hidden by cloud. As he climbed down, I implored him to send me word every day, every hour, every minute.

"Will we ever see each other again?" I asked.

Standing on the ground below, just as he had that first night we met, my love shouted, "Of course! One day we will tell these stories and laugh at everything we went through to be together!"

But though his voice was bright, Romeo looked weary. He was pale with dark circles under his eyes. Staring down at him, I suddenly had a vision that he was dead in his grave, about to be covered in earth.

Perhaps hoping he would cheer me, I told him my fears. He did not laugh this time but said I looked pale, too. Sorrow drinks our blood, he told me. Then, without a last kiss, he called adieu and ran for his life.

I returned to my room to find you there, Mother. I felt nervous seeing you, because it was far earlier than when you usually awoke.

I told you I was not feeling well—which was no lie. I had not slept and I felt quite faint. All I wanted was to get back into bed, pull the covers over my head, and sleep until Romeo came back.

Mother, you thought I was still mourning for Tybalt. Was it your own grief that made you so impatient with mine? In a sharp voice, you said that some grief showed love but other grief was just self-indulgence. Did I think I could wash Tybalt from his grave with tears?

What I *should* weep for, you said, was the fact that Romeo, the villain who murdered Tybalt, was still alive and free. But he wouldn't be for long, you promised.

The sudden change in your attention—from me to Tybalt to Romeo—frightened me. I have always known you had a vengeful side. Indeed, sometimes I think it was more you than Father who pumped life's blood into this feud with the Montagues.

Fearful, I pretended interest in your plan for Romeo to learn what you intended. You said you would send a man to Mantua, where Romeo hid. And with that man, you would send poison to end Romeo's life.

Unsteady in my voice, I asked that you give me this poison so that I could mix in some other ingredients before you sent it. I hinted that these would make the potion even more deadly—when in truth, I meant to pour it out and leave only water in the bottle. Smoothing my hair, you murmured that if I found the poison, you would find the man to deliver it.

In short, you promised killing to comfort me. Mother, mother, is everything in our life to be killing? Is it any wonder so many young people are dead?

But then you changed the subject again. You told me you had news of a sudden joy that would relieve my grief.

Stupidly, I imagined a journey of some kind, a pilgrimage. On such a journey, I might meet Romeo in secret. Why, I might plan many such pilgrimages! One a month . . .

But then you revealed your news. I was to be married to Paris on Thursday—only two days from now. I had been so happily dreaming of my pilgrimages, it took a moment to understand. The very same night that Romeo came to me, Paris came to you. And you agreed to marry me to him—when I had met him but once.

So much for your concerns over whether I could like

him! So much for thinking thirteen too soon to marry. I had suspected it was never my choice, but to have my feelings pushed aside—and then be expected to be happy and grateful!

Rage and horror made me blunt. I swore by Saint Peter that I would not be married on Thursday to Paris—a man who had spent no time wooing me, yet meant to marry me! I shouted that I would rather marry Romeo—whom I professed to hate—than marry Paris.

I think you have never seen me angry, Mother. You did not know quite what to do. The only stinging rebuke you offered was that I should give this news to Father.

Which cheered me some. Father, you have been a fond parent. I know Mother thinks you spoil me. When she accuses you of indulgence, you may scold for a moment—but then you give in. Perhaps I have taken advantage at times, crying for some pretty thing I did not truly need or to escape punishment for a moment of willfulness. But this time, I was sincere. You were my last desperate hope not to marry a man I did not love. And indeed, I had reason to be hopeful, for you had always said that thirteen was too young to marry.

Mother, you took it upon yourself to give Father the news, telling him in short, ugly terms that I would not accept Paris as my husband. I heard it almost as a dare: *See how ungrateful she is, how willful, how proud. Be a proper father, for once!*

And, Father, you did get angry. I've never seen you so angry. Perhaps you imagined that you would come to find me tearstained but smiling, rescued from my grief by your wonderful news. Were you hurt that I rejected your gift? Or perhaps it was my mother's goading? Or the loss of Tybalt and the censure of the prince? Whatever the cause, you had never screamed at me as you did that morning. I should be proud, you bellowed, unworthy as I was, that you had found so worthy a gentleman to be my husband!

Your explosion scared me. I stammered that I was not proud but thankful. And that even though I hated what you offered, I knew it was offered with love.

But you were lost in rage, calling me "chop logic" and "mistress minion," "baggage" and "green-sickness carrion." If I refused to marry Paris on Thursday, you would drag me to the church doors yourself.

I fell on my knees to beg you to listen, but you did not hear me. For the first time I could remember, you showed me your fists, imitating me in a horrible whine: "I'll not wed, I cannot love, I am too young . . ." till I was on the verge of shouting, *I am not too young, I do love, and I have already wed!* Would you have me live in a state of mortal sin, married to two men at once?

For I could not expect Romeo never to hear of this marriage. News traveled back and forth between Verona and Mantua. What if he came to claim me? What would the prince do to a girl who brought shame to his house by marrying his kinsman, when she was already married?

Or—I thought—even worse: What if Romeo, hearing of the marriage, thought I no longer loved him? His wife, who had begged him to send news every hour, goes off and weds someone else within the week. What would he think?

But I couldn't say any of this to you, Father. I was too frightened. Your threats grew so wild, Nurse told you you were wrong to shout at me this way. You swung the fists toward her, told her to stick with her gossip and not interfere with important matters.

But Nurse held firm, insisting she spoke no treason. From down on my knees, I thought, At least there is one who cares for me and will take my part. Mother, even you were shocked by the storm in my father you had provoked.

My pleas for time to mourn Tybalt, time to know Paris better, went unheard. It came down to this choice: I would either marry Paris or I would be disowned. Even in the confusion of that morning, I coldly noted that you who were so proud of the name Capulet were quick to snatch it away from me. You who always said I should not marry too young, that I could marry a man who pleased me—now you were ready to disown me and throw me into the street, to beg, starve or die, you cared not.

And, Mother, when I turned to you for help, you said I could do as I wanted, you were done with me.

So, in that instant, my parents, I decided that I was done with you, too. If the name of Capulet could be taken away from me by my own parents in such a cruel manner—well, its loss was nothing to weep for. Clearly, it was more precious to you than I ever was.

How long did I lie crying on the floor? How long did I struggle to escape the truth that I was about to be double married, and that I would live with my false husband for the rest of my days and never see my true husband again?

Then, Nurse, I became aware of your large, soft, comforting presence. I threw myself onto your lap. "Nurse, what should I do? Am I being punished by heaven for my marriage?

Please, tell me what to do. Some comfort . . ."

And what did you say? This next is hard to remember without bitterness. For so long, you were a true friend. Everything I did and felt and thought, you knew. When I wanted to know the name of the boy in the blue mask, you discovered it. When I needed word from Romeo, you went to him for me. You brought the ropes that let him climb to my rooms. You kept watch while we met in secret. We could not have shared half our love without you.

Yet when I needed you most, you offered only this advice: I should forget Romeo and marry Paris.

Oh, you made your reasons clear. It was all so calm and reasonable. Romeo could not come back to Verona to claim me. In fact, he could not return to Verona at all, except in secrecy. So, what good was he to me?

And so, why not be married to Paris?

Choked with disbelief, I said nothing. And you wittered on, saying how lovely Paris was, such a gentleman! Romeo, pah, he was nothing. My second marriage would be much better than my first. (You seemed to overlook the state of mortal sin I would be living in.)

You, who had always been so loyal to my love for Romeo, now threw that love and loyalty aside without a second thought. And expected me to do the same.

Wanting to give you a chance to take it back, I asked, "Do you speak from your heart?"

"From my heart and soul, too," you said.

Nurse, if you had said, *No, not from my heart, love, but from what must be,* I might have forgiven you. But you pretended these were your true feelings. You spoke, you said, not just from your heart, but your soul. Which showed me you had no heart and no soul.

In that time, when my parents had told me they wished me dead or disowned, when my beloved friend and nurse had transferred all her former affections with such slippery ease, I gained a dark understanding. Most people, I realized, do not truly love. Their devotions are worthless, their loyalties shifting and useless, their attachments based on greed and self-aggrandizement.

Nurse, in trying to reason me out of loving Romeo, you only made me love him the more. He was the only one in my life I loved, because he was the only one in my life who truly knew what love was. All the rest were liars.

I had talked of death before, toyed with the notion of "ending it all." But kneeling on the floor, my throat and head aching, I realized that life without Romeo was no life at all. I had a choice. It was life with Romeo . . .

Or death.

Since no one was true or loyal to me, I felt no pangs in lying. No one would know my heart from now on, except the one person to whom it belonged.

Sniffing, I said, "I feel better now. Tell my mother I am going to Friar Laurence to ask forgiveness for my disobedience."

"Oh, this is my wise girl," you cried.

I smiled. And said nothing. For I was wiser than you realized.

I took with me a knife hidden in my cloak. Why, exactly, I was not sure. Only that I wanted some instrument, some weapon, to make my will a reality should the friar fail me as everyone else had.

As I went, I passed some youths idling in the streets. Their eyes kept watch for anyone who might attack—or be attacked. Their fingers toyed with their swords.

In that moment, I felt what those boys felt. That hunger for what cannot be taken back. The moment that changes everything. So much of life is the same. Hour to hour, day to day. We sleep, we eat, we pray. We welcome new life, let old life out. How do we make our mark upon the world? What can we point to and say, Yes, that's mine?

For me, there was only one thing and the world was trying to take him away from me. I wanted to do something desperate, something true, that would make everyone understand that I was not a child to be pushed into a life simply because it suited everyone else. If I had no other power, I could at least kill myself.

As I approached the chapel, I could not help but remember the last time I had been here. Just the day before, I had raced here a maid eager to be married. Now I arrived a wife without a husband.

Yesterday, the first face I saw here had been Romeo's. But by some hideous joke, today, the first man I saw at the chapel was Paris! He was there, making the arrangements for our wedding, of all things!

The arrogant count greeted me, saying, "Ah, my lady and my wife."

This was a sharp reminder to me that as far as everyone was concerned, my desires were of no matter in this business. Short tempered, I said, "We are not married yet, sir."

He wasn't bothered in the slightest, saying, "But we will be on Thursday. Are you here to make your confession?"

As if my morals were any of his concern!

I said, "If I answer that, then I am confessing to you that I have sins to confess." Which you have no right to know, I thought.

"Well, do not deny to the friar that you love me," said the count, smiling.

He was so bold, so enamored of himself, I might have laughed if I hadn't been so miserable. "I will confess to you that I love the friar very much," I said.

Seeing that his peacock ways had not won me, he tried to be caring, tutting over my tearstained face.

I snapped, "Sir, my face is so plain, a few tears will not mar it."

"Ah, but your face is mine now," said the unbearable creature. "I forbid you to say anything against it."

My hand was on the dagger, ready to slash my cheek, when Friar Laurence—sensing my desperation—approached to tell Paris that he and I must be alone now for my confession. Paris said pompously he would not disturb our devotions.

As he left, he assured me he would come to claim me— early!—on Thursday. And insisted on kissing me. I thought, That will be the last kiss you ever give me.

Running to the back of the chapel, I begged the holy father shut the door.

"Then come weep with me," I said. "I am past all help and hope."

Gently, he said, "Poor child. I see no way to postpone this marriage."

Taking the knife from my cloak, I put it to my throat. "If we cannot postpone it," I said, "I will prevent it. Father, you joined my hand with Romeo's; God joined our hearts. I'll die rather than betray him with another man."

But, really, what could this humble priest do? Bring Romeo back to me? Banish Paris? Change the laws of God and man? The only remedy to my problems lay in my hand. I steadied the knife and tried to will my hands to plunge it into my throat. But if I felt brave about death, I did not yet feel brave about pain. Wincing at the bite of the blade against my skin, I trembled at the thought of what it would feel like to thrust it through the flesh and sinew of my neck. Would I choke on my own blood? Faint as it flowed from my body? How long before I died? It might not be quick. . . .

The friar took hold of the knife and pulled it from my hand. "There is hope," he said quietly. "But only if you truly have the courage to kill yourself."

Wild now, I assured him I did, naming all manner of self-destruction. I would throw myself off a tower, chain myself with bears, walk with serpents. I would do all of this and more to spare myself the sin of betraying my husband with another man.

"Then," said the friar, "do this: Go home. Be merry. Say you will marry Paris on Thursday."

Thinking he meant to gentle me into marriage as the nurse had tried to do, I protested. But he held up a hand and I was silenced.

"Then the night before the wedding, be sure to go to bed alone. Send your nurse away. Then . . ."

At this, the friar went to his chambers and returned with a small clay bottle. Holding it above me, he said that when I was alone in my bed, I should drink the contents. Thinking he had seen my cowardice with the knife and meant to give me kinder means of self-destruction, I nodded eagerly and reached for the bottle.

But he held it out of my hands. "When you have drunk it, you will feel drowsy. Your pulse will slow, then stop. Your cheeks will grow pale, your limbs stiff and cold. To all the world, you will *appear* dead.

"But you will not be dead. In less than two days, you will wake up, feeling rested as if from a long sleep. And by that time, your family, thinking you dead, will have buried you in the Capulet family crypt. In the meantime, I will send word to Romeo in Mantua, telling him about our plan. I will tell him he is to come to the tomb by night. So that when you awake, you and he can run away together."

Hearing this plan, I cried, "Give it to me, give it to me!" and snatched at the bottle as if it were hope itself.

Handing it to me at last, the friar cautioned, "You must be strong, resolute, for this is no easy thing to do."

"Love will give me strength," I said. Because what fear should I have when suddenly everything that I thought was lost was possible again? This plain little bottle contained all my happiness. Wrapping it in my robes, I bade the dear friar farewell and ran from the chapel.

I was quite the actress when I returned home that afternoon. I walked right into the preparations for the wedding. Servants were rushing here and there. Father, you were checking the guest list, the food, making sure everything was to your liking. I thought of what would become of your fancy wedding feast and smiled. Remember, Nurse? You remarked on my merry mood. I was merry. I would die soon.

Father, you greeted me with, How now, my headstrong! Where have you been? Which was my cue to recite the speech I had rehearsed on my way home. I deeply repented my sin of disobedience. Father Laurence had told me to lay myself at your feet—which I did, and nicely, too—and beg your pardon. From now on, I mumbled to your shoes, I would be ruled by you.

You were so pleased, Father! Clapping your hands, you declared the wedding would be held tomorrow instead. Go, someone, you shouted, and tell the count.

With secret spite, I continued to perform my part of dutiful daughter. I told you I had already seen the count and showed him much affection, all within the bounds of maidenly modesty, of course!

This made you so happy you allowed me up off my knees. You announced that you were much indebted to this wise friar, indeed the whole city was. I heartily agreed. If only you knew how much the friar had truly done for me.

Knowing I was about to leave this life behind, I took pleasure in pretending pleasantness to those who had so hurt me. So, Nurse, I said I wanted your advice on which robes and jewels I should wear tomorrow. You have always liked dressing me up, so you were well satisfied.

Mother, only you were uneasy. Were you jealous that I asked the nurse and not you? Or did a mother's intuition tell you that this was no true obedience but a pretense? If you thought so, you said nothing.

Nurse, did you enjoy that last day? It was just like the day of the feast. I should wear the red, no, red was not suitable for brides. Blue—but blue wasn't my best color. Green, should it be the green again? Thinking I would like to be buried in the dress I wore when I met Romeo, I said, Yes, I felt I looked my very best in green.

We did not speak of Romeo at all. It was as if I had never met him, as if I had only danced with Paris the night of the feast, liked him well, and now we were to be married. Just as everyone had planned and wanted. Nurse, you said several times how good it was that everything had gone as it should. Did you really think so, Nurse? Or did you hope to wish it into being the truth? I am not sure, even now.

As happy as you were to assemble my bridal finery, you were not so happy that night when I told you I wished to sleep alone for my final night at home. You knew, I whispered, better than anyone, of my sinful state. I wanted to pray to God to show me mercy.

Mother, you, too, had to be banished. I think your anxiety grew as night approached. And as always, you were reluctant to give up an opportunity to tell me what to do. Was everything ready? you asked. Did I need anything else? Yes and no, I said.

Your last words to me were that I should go to sleep, for I needed it, a mixture of care and nagging that was fitting for our last exchange.

Farewell, I said.

And now, as I sit upon my bed and scratch these words, I say another farewell. I shall leave this letter hidden in the chest you have packed for me, to take with me as I begin my new life with Paris. Hopefully, days, even weeks from now, you will unpack it and find this letter. Then, shall you finally know the daughter you lost. And why you lost her.

I have confessed to you that I am not truly dead—but I shall be dead to you when this is over. We shall likely never see each other again.

The little vial sits beside me on the bed, its cork snug. All I have to do is pluck the cork from its mouth, raise it to mine and I am free.

But I am not quite ready for freedom yet. As angry as I am with all of you, now on the verge of leaving you, I feel sad. I hope one day you think well of me—and even of my husband. Neither of us meant this to happen. We did not mean to cause you sorrow. I swear to you, when we met and loved, I did not know who he was. I swear it.

But . . . even as I say this, I think, Why does it matter? Why must I swear? I cannot say if I could spare you the sorrow, I would have everything undone. Perhaps love has made me a little cruel. But hate and pride have made others far crueler.

Father, Mother—you have both told me, girls much younger than I become mothers. Yes, and they become widows, too. Become mourners at their own sons' funerals. They go from maid to crone in a little span, a nothing of time. I have seen them. So much of their life they have given to those who are gone, they are like the dead themselves. A world ruled by men's anger is not a happy place for women. When it is truly my time to die, I wish to remember something that was once mine.

I am sick of this war. I want no part in it.

Romeo wants no part in it, either, though you will say he has played a part—and a deadly one—already. But that is where this quarrel takes us. It makes murderers or corpses of all of us. Since we cannot be Capulets and Montagues and be at peace, we shall cease to be Capulet and Montague.

I think now about the things I will never know.

I will never have children who live in the wealth I have known.

Never manage a great house.

Never serve as gracious hostess to princes.

But neither shall I lose my children to vengeance. Neither shall I see my house wrecked by hatred. Neither shall those princes rail against my family for destroying the peace.

There is so much I have not done. But I have loved and been loved. And in this new, unknown land, I feel certain I will know love still.

So do not grieve.

I pick up the vial the friar gave me. It is the one thing in this world that will help me be with Romeo. And yet I am reluctant to drink it. Even the semblance of death feels too near to it to be safe. Coward's doubts creep into my head. What if the friar had mixed the potion in haste and made it too strong?

Or what if, fearing punishment for his part in our marriage, he thinks to silence me by killing me? No, he would not do such a thing. He is a good man.

But I have thought other people good and learned otherwise too late.

Now my mind is fixed on fear. What if I awake before Romeo comes and I am left alone in the crypt? What if there is no air and I cannot breathe? I shall suffocate, and Romeo will come to find me truly dead.

Or what if he cannot open the door to the tomb, and I am trapped to starve?

The dead. I had not thought about them. I shall be there alone with them. With Tybalt, who, just laid in the vault, shall still have some meat upon him. Bare, yellowed bones are fearful enough, but a rotting corpse is much worse. I do not want to see my cousin that way, eyes fallen, cheeks spotted with mold. And yet they will lay me right next to him. Shall we touch? Shall the worms that feed on him mistake me for truly dead and crawl upon my flesh?

I may go mad. The stench alone may make me mad.

No. Back, fear. The friar warned me of the perils of giving you power. It is a terrible thing I must do. But even more terrible is losing Romeo.

But I still see Tybalt before me, as if I shall shortly join him, not just in the vault, but in the afterlife. He reaches for me, whispers that we are kin: both Capulet and both dead . . .

No! I will not fear. Romeo, I shall think on Romeo.

Romeo, I drink to thee. . . .

Epilogue

A few months later, a gentleman came across an elderly woman wandering and lost on the road. Her clothes were ragged, her manner vague. When he asked how she came to be in such a place, she wailed, She's dead! She's dead. My poor lady's dead.

It came out that she had once been a nursemaid to a great family in Verona. For the past fourteen years, her job had been the care of their only daughter, a girl called Juliet.

Intrigued by her story and worried for her safety, the gentleman took the old woman to a tavern and gave her something to eat. As she ate—and drank—she told her story. "A sweeter babe you never saw, sir. When she sucked, she'd look up at me with two big gray eyes, and I'd whisper, 'You're a wise one, my little love. A wise and virtuous one—and you'll grow to be a great lady.'"

The old woman drank deep. "But she never did, sir. She died before she had her chance."

Intrigued, the gentleman asked how had the poor girl died? What was it that killed her?

"Love, sir. Oh, it was love. And hate. Love and hate both . . ."

You've heard of the feud between the Capulets and Montagues, sir? It's lasted for ages, generations have fought and died in it. No one knows what caused the feud. Isn't that strange, sir, how folk will fight and have no idea what they're fighting for? If you asked me to kill or die, believe me, I'd want to know why.

At any rate, it's finished now. The great feud's over. But it took the deaths of six people to do it. Ruined the families as well. Montagues, Capulets—the heirs are all dead. Both family lines are finished.

Juliet died on her wedding day. She was to be married to the count Paris. He was mad for her. At first, I thought he was only mad for her father's money. But I was wrong about him. He loved my lady after all—little good it did him.

What was I saying? Oh. So, the night before she was to be married, Juliet sent me away. Well, I should have known then, sir. Every night since her birth, I've stayed with her. Now, all of a sudden, she didn't want me? I should have thought.

She had cause to be sad, you see. For she loved another lad. A Montague. Which was sorrow enough. But only the day before, he'd been banished for the murder of her cousin Tybalt. Maybe you heard about that as well.

And the other thing was, she couldn't get married to the count—not truly. Because she'd already married her Romeo in secret. And I helped her to do it. Because she was my lamb. What she wanted, I wanted. That's how it was, always. If you have children, sir, you know. Nothing makes you happy like making them happy.

Maybe it was addled of me. If my husband were alive, he'd have said, Are you mad? You go straight to her parents. No good'll come of this. He'd have been right, too. Ah, well, no point thinking "should haves" now.

Her parents told her she was to marry Paris right after Tybalt was killed. I suppose they meant well. They thought she was heartbroken over her cousin, when, of course, it was the man who killed him she was heartbroken over. They thought, We'll marry her off, start her having babies, she'll forget about all this.

The day they told her to marry Paris. Oh, it was terrible! Juliet, poor thing, was terrified. Here she was already married and her parents were telling her she must marry someone else. She shouted no, she wouldn't do it. She was right in a way, but how were they to know? Her mother turned cold on her immediately. She was a hard-hearted lady, sir. If it'd not been for me, Juliet'd never known motherly affection.

Then my lady's father came in. Now, he was a good man, sir, kind. At least he was then. And he doted on Juliet—you never saw a father loved a child so. But when Juliet said she wouldn't marry the count, after all he'd done to arrange things, he flew into a temper. Well, I suppose it would have been a great embarrassment to him, for the count was related to the prince himself.

He shouted that he'd disown Juliet, throw her out. Poor girl was on her knees, begging for just a little time. But her parents would have none of it. It was marriage or disgrace.

Well, it got so bad, I had to step in. I told my lord Capulet he was wrong to shout at Juliet when she was so grieved already. Because I knew, sir, once he had time to think, he'd regret the things he was saying. He was that kind of man. Loud talk, soft heart.

But what do you think? He started shouting at me. I told him to his face, I speak no treason. After all the years I've served with them, I'm not allowed to speak my piece?

They left Juliet at her wit's end. Wailing on the floor, saying she wanted to die. Eyes swollen, cheeks wet with tears, she looked at me and asked, What should I do?

And I thought, Well, what can she do? She has to marry Paris.

I never meant to be cruel, sir. I knew she loved Romeo. But Romeo was gone, wasn't he? He couldn't come back. He was as good as dead as far as she was concerned. Which made her as good as a widow. Now, I'm a widow, sir, and it's no life for a young girl. She ought to have had children of her own, a . . .

. Forgive me, sir, it's so hard to think on. I had a daughter once. Susan. She never had her chance, either.

What I mean is, I was thinking of Juliet when I told her to forget all about Romeo and marry the count. She didn't have a choice. She couldn't go against her family, not without a husband to help her. I tried to make it seem as if I thought it was a good match for her. Maybe I said some things I shouldn't have about Romeo, but . . . it was for her own good that I said them.

She just looked at me with those great gray eyes and asked if I spoke from my heart. I said I did, and my soul, too. For I'd never spoken to her any other way. I didn't want her to think me a liar now.

She murmured that she was much comforted. Which was a comfort to me, I can tell you. She went to church that afternoon, came back all smiles and sweetness. Oh, yes, she would marry the count. She was sorry she'd been so wild and stubborn.

She even asked me to help her pick out her wedding clothes. I'd never had the chance to do that for my child. And as we did, we chatted away just as we always did. At least I thought. But now as I remember, it was me telling my stories. Juliet just smiled. And it wasn't her smile, sir, I should have seen that. Her true smile would turn midnight to morning, it was that bright. This was a secret smile.

And then she said she didn't want me to stay with her that night.

I didn't feel good about it, but like I said, what she wanted, I wanted. I felt sad as I went away. I thought it was just the sadness you feel when the chick leaves the nest. A good sadness, if you like. I even cried a bit, to make myself feel better.

The next morning, when I went to get her, I bustled in, talking away to her like most mornings. Calling her lamb, lady, sweetheart. When I saw she was still asleep, I teased her, calling her a slug-a-bed. I teased her that she best get up before the count arrived or she'd have a rude awakening.

I pulled back the curtains, then went to look at her. Well, not only was she still asleep, she was still in her clothes from the day before. The green dress lay at the foot of the bed. That's odd, I thought, and gave her a little nudge.

But when I touched her, I knew. For she was cold, sir. Still and cold.

Do you have children, sir? No? Well, then you can only try to imagine her parents' sorrow. And shock! Hard enough when they go like my Susan, after an illness. But Juliet, so full of life just the day before, and now dead on her wedding day. Her parents thought it must be the grief of Tybalt's death that carried her off. (I must confess, I knew Romeo was the true reason for her broken heart.) The poor count, he had just arrived to find out death had claimed his bride before he even took her to the altar.

Probably we'd be there wailing still if it hadn't been for the priest. He was the one who told us we must now take everything we'd done for the wedding and turn it into a funeral. The music, the flowers, all of it. At the time, I thought, Well, good to keep folk busy when tragedy comes. You don't let them think too much.

But what we didn't know, sir, was that there was a reason the friar moved so quickly on the funeral. It was the same reason for my lady's secret smile the night before.

For she wasn't dead at all, sir. The priest had given her a potion to make her lie like the dead for a time. And in that time, he meant to send Romeo a letter that his lady wife lay in the vault, and he should collect her there and take her away.

If he were alive, my husband, Robert, would have told the priest the same as he would have told me. Don't meddle. Everyone has their fate and the more people try to avoid it, the more trouble they get into.

For, sir, on that road to Mantua, that letter was lost. A plague had kept the messenger indoors. The priest's letter never reached Romeo.

Now, who sent that plague, sir? Fate.

And fate was even more cruel. Because Romeo's servant happened to see Juliet's funeral procession. Faithful servant that he was, he took the news to Romeo that his Juliet was dead. Romeo immediately got on his horse and made haste back to Verona.

On his way, he bought poison. From an apothecary too poor to say no to him, even though the penalty for selling death is death.

These young things, sir. Their hearts are so soft, so easily broken. They feel too much. We old ones, we're too tired to feel like that. We've done most of our living. We know that most things aren't all good or bad. Life's what you make of it. But young ones don't know that yet. They're greedy, not in a bad way, sir. But they don't know you don't get your reward in this life. You can't hold any one person too close. I know.

When I lost my Susan, I thought I'd go mad. But I came out of it. Life was . . . grayer somehow. I never cared about anything in the same way. My heart went quiet. And when I lost my Robert, it went even quieter.

But I don't think about it. Maybe I talk a bit too much, so I don't hear the quiet in my heart, but you can understand that, can't you, sir? But these young things, when they lose someone . . . sometimes they don't have the strength to bear it.

Now, if fate were kind, my lady would have awakened before Romeo arrived. He'd have found her frightened out of her wits waking up surrounded by the dead—but still among the living herself. If fate were kind, the priest who, hearing his letter had not been read by Romeo was hurrying to the crypt, would have arrived in time.

But fate is not kind, sir. Fate does as she pleases.

For when my lady woke up, there lay her love, Romeo, dead on the floor. The apothecary's poison was still in his hand. I warrant he died happy, thinking he was going to his Juliet.

Can you imagine it, sir? All she'd done—getting the potion, drinking it, having the courage to wake up in that awful place. She'd turned down marriage with the count, turned her back on her family and everything she knew. All for Romeo. And now he was dead at her feet. For so long, she'd hoped fate would let them be together. Now, it was truly the end.

By this time the priest had come. And the guard was around, keeping an eye out for grave robbers. Knowing they'd want answers if they caught him there, the priest was in no mood to stay. He tried to get Juliet to go with him, saying he'd put her in a nunnery.

After all my telling, sir, you know my lady well enough to know she wouldn't go.

I imagine my poor girl in that awful place. The only sweet living thing in it. Nearby would have been her cousin Tybalt—a gallant man, no matter what they say of his temper, he was always kind to me. But death has a keen appetite, sir. I shudder to think what work the worms had done by the time my girl saw him.

But perhaps she took no notice. Perhaps she only had eyes for Romeo. Perhaps she only thought of what she was about to do.

He must have drunk all the poison, because that's not how she ended herself. No. They found her with his knife buried in her heart. If you'd ever seen her, sir, you'd know. She was a tiny thing. She had lovely delicate hands. Snow white, they fluttered like doves in the air when she was happy or excited.

It must have taken great strength to . . .

Or maybe it took no strength at all to push the knife

home. Maybe her poor heart was already so broken, it took but a scratch to stop it beating. Without Romeo, she wanted so much to leave this life. There, I suppose, you might say fate was kind.

They found her lying across him, like the newlyweds they were, a stone vault for a wedding bed, warm blood for warm sheets. They'd found peace at last.

Don't tell me any sermons, sir, on the sin of suicide. I won't hear it. Because for all the poison and knives, Juliet and Romeo didn't kill themselves. We did. We killed them with our feuds and our lies and our pride. So don't tell me they can't lie in hallowed ground. Innocent, that's what they were. Innocent and good. Too good for this evil place.

Oh, forgive me, sir, I don't know what I'm saying half the time. I confess, sometimes from sorrow, I drown what wits I have left. But you're a kind gentleman, I see that. You wouldn't take an old lady to task for it.

What then? Well, like the prince said, some were pardoned, some punished. And I don't have to tell you, do I, the rich are seldom punished in this world. (Although I can't speak for the next.) They hung that poor apothecary that sold Romeo the poison.

The Montagues and the Capulets ended their feud. The Montagues promised to build a fine gold statue to Juliet. The Capulets said they'd do the same for Romeo. I'm sure it's beautiful, but I can't help thinking, maybe if they'd thought less of their wealth and more of their children . . .

No, that's unkind of me. For they were punished, sir. Punished hard. What greater punishment is there than life when you've lost everything that made it worth living? Lady

Montague never knew of her son's death. She died of grief over his exile, the very same day he died. Old Capulet died just two months later.

Paris, sir? Oh, his was a sad end. Like I said, he did love Juliet after all. When my lady died—or when we thought she had—he took himself to her tomb that same night. But you can guess who he found there. That's right, sir. Romeo. One told the other, You've no right to be here. But both refused to go. Romeo was desperate, poor lad. There was a fight and he killed Paris. They found him there, lying with the others. I suppose it was fitting in a way.

Friar Laurence did all right, at least as far as any formal punishment was concerned. The prince believed him when he said he'd tried to act in the best interests of the peace. He thought if he married a Montague to a Capulet, maybe the two houses would stop their fighting. So the prince left him alone. He never forgave himself, though. Sometimes we punish ourselves the worst.

My lady Capulet never forgave me. She blamed me for all of it, for what I did to help Juliet be with Romeo. I should have told her, she said—as if she'd ever done a thing for her child's happiness. And when her husband died, she threw me out. Twenty years I was with their family, and they just threw me out like that. I'd say I could see it from her side, but I can't. Pointing fingers at me when . . . They say grief hardens the heart, but I can't say I believe it of her. Her heart was always hard.

When you try to figure out who killed whom, who started it, who was to blame—you can't. It's too tangled. All you can do is think of the ones who died. Romeo, Juliet, Tybalt. Lady

Montague. That young gentleman Tybalt killed—Mercutio. And Paris. All of them dead over a quarrel—and no one can even remember what the quarrel was about. Like the past killed the future. Or maybe it's just fate again, up to her dirty tricks.

So you see, sir, it doesn't pay to set too much store by any one person or thing in this life. If I'd done that, I'd have been dead many years ago. Mind you, I shan't last much longer. Gets to a point where too many have gone before you. My child, husband . . .

And my other child. She was a daughter to me, Juliet. I hope she wouldn't mind me saying it.

I regret. . . .

Well, that's what we say, isn't it, sir? When your children find sorrow in this world and you can't help them. I regret. What I did. What I didn't do. As if what we do makes any difference in this world.

I do thank you for your kindness to an old woman. I hope for your pains, you shall never know such woes as I have.

Romeo & Juliet

by William Shakespeare

DRAMATIS PERSONAE

CHORUS.

ESCALUS, Prince of Verona.

PARIS, a young Count, kinsman to the Prince.

MONTAGUE, nobleman, head of a feuding Veronese family.

CAPULET, nobleman, head of a feuding Veronese family.

AN OLD MAN, of the Capulet family.

ROMEO, son to Montague.

TYBALT, nephew to Lady Capulet.

MERCUTIO, kinsman to the Prince and friend to Romeo.

BENVOLIO, nephew to Montague and friend to Romeo.

TYBALT, nephew to Lady Capulet.

FRIAR LAURENCE, Franciscan.

FRIAR JOHN, Franciscan.

BALTHASAR, servant to Romeo.

ABRAM, servant to Montague.

SAMPSON, servant to Capulet.

GREGORY, servant to Capulet.

PETER, servant to Juliet's nurse.

AN APOTHECARY.

THREE MUSICIANS.

AN OFFICER.

LADY MONTAGUE, wife to Montague.

LADY CAPULET, wife to Capulet.

JULIET, daughter to Capulet.

NURSE to Juliet.

CITIZENS OF VERONA: Gentlemen and
Gentlewomen of both houses, Maskers,
Torchbearers, Pages, Guards, Watchmen,
Servants, and Attendants.

SCENE: *Verona and Mantua.*

PROLOGUE

Enter CHORUS.

CHORUS

Two households, both alike in dignity,

In fair Verona, where we lay our scene,

From ancient grudge break to new mutiny,

Where civil blood makes civil hands unclean.

From forth the fatal loins of these two foes

A pair of star-cross'd lovers take their life;

Whose misadventur'd piteous overthrows

Doth with their death bury their parents' strife.

The fearful passage of their death-mark'd love,

And the continuance of their parents' rage,

Which, but their children's end, naught could

    remove,

Is now the two hours' traffic of our stage;

The which if you with patient ears attend,

What here shall miss, our toil shall strive to mend.

Exit.

ACT I.

SCENE I.

VERONA. *A public place.*

Enter SAMPSON *and* GREGORY *(with swords and bucklers)*
of the house of Capulet.

SAMPSON

Gregory, on my word, we'll not carry coals.

GREGORY

No, for then we should be colliers.

SAMPSON

I mean, an we be in choler, we'll draw.

GREGORY

Ay, while you live, draw your neck out of collar.

SAMPSON

I strike quickly, being moved.

GREGORY

But thou art not quickly moved to strike.

SAMPSON

A dog of the house of Montague moves me.

GREGORY

To move is to stir, and to be valiant is to stand.
Therefore, if thou art moved, thou runn'st
away.

SAMPSON

A dog of that house shall move me to stand.
I will take the wall of any man or maid of
Montague's.

GREGORY

That shows thee a weak slave; for the weakest goes to the wall.

SAMPSON

'Tis true; and therefore women, being the weaker vessels, are ever thrust to the wall. Therefore I will push Montague's men from the wall and thrust his maids to the wall.

GREGORY

The quarrel is between our masters and us their men.

SAMPSON

'Tis all one. I will show myself a tyrant. When I have fought with the men, I will be cruel with the maids—I will cut off their heads.

GREGORY

The heads of the maids?

SAMPSON

Ay, the heads of the maids, or their maidenheads.
Take it in what sense thou wilt.

GREGORY

They must take it in sense that feel it.

SAMPSON

Me they shall feel while I am able to stand; and
'tis known I am a pretty piece of flesh.

GREGORY

'Tis well thou art not fish; if thou hadst, thou
hadst been poor-John. Draw thy tool! Here
comes two of the house of Montagues.

Enter two other Servingmen, ABRAM *and* BALTHASAR.

SAMPSON

My naked weapon is out. Quarrel! I will back
thee.

GREGORY

How? turn thy back and run?

SAMPSON

Fear me not.

GREGORY

No, marry. I fear thee!

SAMPSON

Let us take the law of our sides; let them begin.

GREGORY

I will frown as I pass by, and let them take it as
they list.

SAMPSON

Nay, as they dare. I will bite my thumb at them;
which is disgrace to them, if they bear it.

ABRAM

Do you bite your thumb at us, sir?

SAMPSON

I do bite my thumb, sir.

ABRAM

Do you bite your thumb at us, sir?

SAMPSON

[aside to GREGORY*]* Is the law of our side if I say ay?

GREGORY

[aside to SAMPSON*]* No.

SAMPSON

No, sir, I do not bite my thumb at you, sir; but I bite my thumb, sir.

GREGORY

Do you quarrel, sir?

ABRAM

Quarrel, sir? No, sir.

SAMPSON

But if you do, sir, I am for you. I serve as good a
man as you.

ABRAM

No better.

SAMPSON

Well, sir.

Enter BENVOLIO.

GREGORY

[aside to SAMPSON*]* Say "better." Here comes one of
my master's kinsmen.

SAMPSON

Yes, better, sir.

ABRAM
You lie.

SAMPSON
Draw, if you be men. Gregory, remember thy
swashing blow. *[They fight.]*

BENVOLIO
Part, fools! *[Beats down their swords.]*
Put up your swords. You know not what you do.

Enter TYBALT.

TYBALT
What, art thou drawn among these heartless
    hinds?
Turn thee Benvolio! look upon thy death.

BENVOLIO

I do but keep the peace. Put up thy sword,
Or manage it to part these men with me.

TYBALT

What, drawn, and talk of peace? I hate the word
As I hate hell, all Montagues, and thee.
Have at thee, coward! *[They fight.]*

Enter an OFFICER *and three or four* CITIZENS *with clubs
or partisans.*

OFFICER

Clubs, bills, and partisans! Strike! Beat them down!

CITIZENS

Down with the Capulets! Down with the
Montagues!

Enter OLD CAPULET *in his gown and* LADY CAPULET.

CAPULET

What noise is this? Give me my long sword, ho!

LADY CAPULET

A crutch, a crutch! Why call you for a sword?

CAPULET

My sword, I say! Old Montague is come
And flourishes his blade in spite of me.

Enter OLD MONTAGUE *and* LADY MONTAGUE.

MONTAGUE

Thou villain Capulet!—Hold me not, let me go.

LADY MONTAGUE

Thou shalt not stir one foot to seek a foe.

Enter PRINCE ESCALUS, *with his* TRAIN.

PRINCE

Rebellious subjects, enemies to peace,

Profaners of this neighbour-stained steel—

Will they not hear? What, ho! you men, you
beasts,

That quench the fire of your pernicious rage

With purple fountains issuing from your veins!

On pain of torture, from those bloody hands

Throw your mistempered weapons to the ground

And hear the sentence of your moved prince.

Three civil brawls, bred of an airy word

By thee, old Capulet, and Montague,

Have thrice disturb'd the quiet of our streets

And made Verona's ancient citizens

Cast by their grave beseeming ornaments

To wield old partisans, in hands as old,

Cank'red with peace, to part your cank'red hate.

If ever you disturb our streets again,

Your lives shall pay the forfeit of the peace.

For this time all the rest depart away.

You, Capulet, shall go along with me;

And, Montague, come you this afternoon,

To know our farther pleasure in this case,

To old Freetown, our common judgment place.

Once more, on pain of death, all men depart.

Exeunt all but MONTAGUE, LADY MONTAGUE, *and* BENVOLIO.

MONTAGUE

Who set this ancient quarrel new abroach?

Speak, nephew, were you by when it began?

BENVOLIO

Here were the servants of your adversary

And yours, close fighting ere I did approach.

I drew to part them. In the instant came

The fiery Tybalt, with his sword prepar'd;
Which, as he breath'd defiance to my ears,
He swung about his head and cut the winds,
Who, nothing hurt withal, hiss'd him in scorn.
While we were interchanging thrusts and blows,
Came more and more, and fought on part and
    part,
Till the Prince came, who parted either part.

LADY MONTAGUE

O, where is Romeo? Saw you him to-day?
Right glad I am he was not at this fray.

BENVOLIO

Madam, an hour before the worshipp'd sun
Peer'd forth the golden window of the East,
A troubled mind drave me to walk abroad;
Where, underneath the grove of sycamore
That westward rooteth from the city's side,
So early walking did I see your son.

Towards him I made; but he was ware of me
And stole into the covert of the wood.
I—measuring his affections by my own,
Which then most sought where most might not
    be found,
Being one too many by my weary self—
Pursu'd my humour, not pursuing his,
And gladly shunn'd who gladly fled from me.

MONTAGUE
Many a morning hath he there been seen,
With tears augmenting the fresh morning's dew,
Adding to clouds more clouds with his deep
    sighs;
But all so soon as the all-cheering sun
Should in the farthest East begin to draw
The shady curtains from Aurora's bed,
Away from light steals home my heavy son
And private in his chamber pens himself,
Shuts up his windows, locks fair daylight
And makes himself an artificial night.

Black and portentous must this humour prove
Unless good counsel may the cause remove.

BENVOLIO
My noble uncle, do you know the cause?

MONTAGUE
I neither know it nor can learn of him.

BENVOLIO
Have you importun'd him by any means?

MONTAGUE
Both by myself and many other friends;
But he, his own affections' counsellor,
Is to himself—I will not say how true—
But to himself so secret and so close,
So far from sounding and discovery,
As is the bud bit with an envious worm

Ere he can spread his sweet leaves to the air
Or dedicate his beauty to the sun.
Could we but learn from whence his sorrows
   grow,
We would as willingly give cure as know.

Enter ROMEO.

BENVOLIO

See, where he comes. So please you step aside,
I'll know his grievance, or be much denied.

MONTAGUE

I would thou wert so happy by thy stay
To hear true shrift. Come, madam, let's away,

Exeunt MONTAGUE *and* LADY MONTAGUE.

BENVOLIO
Good morrow, cousin.

ROMEO
Is the day so young?

BENVOLIO
But new struck nine.

ROMEO
Ay me! sad hours seem long.
Was that my father that went hence so fast?

BENVOLIO
It was. What sadness lengthens Romeo's hours?

ROMEO

Not having that which having makes them
   short.

BENVOLIO

In love?

ROMEO

Out—

BENVOLIO

Of love?

ROMEO

Out of her favour where I am in love.

BENVOLIO

Alas that love, so gentle in his view,

Should be so tyrannous and rough in proof!

ROMEO

Alas that love, whose view is muffled still,

Should without eyes see pathways to his will!

Where shall we dine? O me! What fray was here?

Yet tell me not, for I have heard it all.

Here's much to do with hate, but more with
love.

Why then, O brawling love! O loving hate!

O anything, of nothing first create!

O heavy lightness! serious vanity!

Misshapen chaos of well-seeming forms!

Feather of lead, bright smoke, cold fire, sick
health!

Still-waking sleep, that is not what it is

This love feel I, that feel no love in this.

Dost thou not laugh?

BENVOLIO

No, coz, I rather weep.

ROMEO

Good heart, at what?

BENVOLIO

At thy good heart's oppression.

ROMEO

Why, such is love's transgression.

Griefs of mine own lie heavy in my breast,

Which thou wilt propagate, to have it prest

With more of thine. This love that thou hast
   shown

Doth add more grief to too much of mine own.

Love is a smoke rais'd with the fume of sighs;

Being purg'd, a fire sparkling in lovers' eyes;

Being vex'd, a sea nourish'd with lovers' tears.

What is it else? A madness most discreet,
A choking gall, and a preserving sweet.
Farewell, my coz.

BENVOLIO
Soft! I will go along.
An if you leave me so, you do me wrong.

ROMEO
Tut! I have lost myself; I am not here:
This is not Romeo, he's some other where.

BENVOLIO
Tell me in sadness, who is that you love?

ROMEO
What, shall I groan and tell thee?

BENVOLIO

Groan? Why, no;
But sadly tell me who.

ROMEO

Bid a sick man in sadness make his will.
Ah, word ill urg'd to one that is so ill!
In sadness, cousin, I do love a woman.

BENVOLIO

I aim'd so near when I suppos'd you lov'd.

ROMEO

A right good markman! And she's fair I love.

BENVOLIO

A right fair mark, fair coz, is soonest hit.

ROMEO

Well, in that hit you miss. She'll not be hit
With Cupid's arrow. She hath Dian's wit,
And, in strong proof of chastity well arm'd,
From Love's weak childish bow she lives
  unharm'd.
She will not stay the siege of loving terms,
Nor bide th' encounter of assailing eyes,
Nor ope her lap to saint-seducing gold.
O, she's rich in beauty; only poor
That, when she dies, with beauty dies her store.

BENVOLIO

Then she hath sworn that she will still live
  chaste?

ROMEO

She hath, and in that sparing makes huge waste;
For beauty, starv'd with her severity,
Cuts beauty off from all posterity.

She is too fair, too wise, wisely too fair,
To merit bliss by making me despair.
She hath forsworn to love, and in that vow
Do I live dead that live to tell it now.

BENVOLIO
Be rul'd by me: forget to think of her.

ROMEO
O, teach me how I should forget to think!

BENVOLIO
By giving liberty unto thine eyes.
Examine other beauties.

ROMEO
'Tis the way
To call hers, exquisite, in question more.

These happy masks that kiss fair ladies' brows,

Being black puts us in mind they hide the fair.

He that is strucken blind cannot forget

The precious treasure of his eyesight lost.

Show me a mistress that is passing fair,

What doth her beauty serve but as a note

Where I may read who pass'd that passing fair?

Farewell. Thou canst not teach me to forget.

BENVOLIO

I'll pay that doctrine, or else die in debt.

Exeunt.

SCENE II.

A street.

Enter CAPULET, COUNTY PARIS, *and* SERVANT—*the*
CLOWN.

CAPULET

But Montague is bound as well as I,
In penalty alike; and 'tis not hard, I think,
For men so old as we to keep the peace.

PARIS

Of honourable reckoning are you both,
And pity 'tis you liv'd at odds so long.
But now, my lord, what say you to my suit?

CAPULET

But saying o'er what I have said before:
My child is yet a stranger in the world,

She hath not seen the change of fourteen years;
Let two more summers wither in their pride
Ere we may think her ripe to be a bride.

PARIS

Younger than she are happy mothers made.

CAPULET

And too soon marr'd are those so early made.
The earth hath swallowed all my hopes but she;
She is the hopeful lady of my earth.
But woo her, gentle Paris, get her heart;
My will to her consent is but a part.
An she agree, within her scope of choice
Lies my consent and fair according voice.
This night I hold an old accustom'd feast,
Whereto I have invited many a guest,
Such as I love; and you among the store,
One more, most welcome, makes my number
    more.

At my poor house look to behold this night
Earth-treading stars that make dark heaven light.
Such comfort as do lusty young men feel
When well apparell'd April on the heel
Of limping Winter treads, even such delight
Among fresh female buds shall you this night
Inherit at my house. Hear all, all see,
And like her most whose merit most shall be;
Which, on more view of many, mine, being one,
May stand in number, though in reck'ning none.
Come, go with me. Go, sirrah, trudge about
Through fair Verona; find those persons out
Whose names are written there, and to them
    say,
My house and welcome on their pleasure stay.

Exeunt CAPULET *and* PARIS.

SERVANT
Find them out whose names are written here?
It is written that the shoemaker should meddle

with his yard and the tailor with his last, the
fisher with his pencil and the painter with his
nets; but I am sent to find those persons whose
names are here writ, and can never find what
names the writing person hath here writ. I must
to the learned. In good time!

Enter BENVOLIO *and* ROMEO.

BENVOLIO
Tut, man, one fire burns out another's burning;
One pain is lessened by another's anguish;
Turn giddy, and be holp by backward turning;
One desperate grief cures with another's
    languish.
Take thou some new infection to thy eye,
And the rank poison of the old will die.

ROMEO
Your plantain leaf is excellent for that.

BENVOLIO
For what, I pray thee?

ROMEO
For your broken shin.

BENVOLIO
Why, Romeo, art thou mad?

ROMEO
Not mad, but bound more than a madman is;
Shut up in prison, kept without my food,
Whipp'd and tormented and—God-den, good
fellow.

SERVANT
God gi' go-den. I pray, sir, can you read?

ROMEO

Ay, mine own fortune in my misery.

SERVANT

Perhaps you have learned it without book. But I
pray, can you read anything you see?

ROMEO

Ay, if I know the letters and the language.

SERVANT

Ye say honestly. Rest you merry!

ROMEO

Stay, fellow; I can read. *[He reads.]*

"Signior Martino and his wife and daughters;
County Anselmo and his beauteous sisters;

The lady widow of Vitruvio;
Signior Placentio and His lovely nieces;
Mercutio and his brother Valentine;
Mine uncle Capulet, his wife, and daughters;
My fair niece Rosaline and Livia;
Signior Valentio and His cousin Tybalt;
Lucio and the lively Helena."
A fair assembly. Whither should they come?

SERVANT
Up.

ROMEO
Whither?

SERVANT
To supper, to our house.

ROMEO

Whose house?

SERVANT

My master's.

ROMEO

Indeed I should have ask'd you that before.

SERVANT

Now I'll tell you without asking. My master is the great rich Capulet; and if you be not of the house of Montagues, I pray come and crush a cup of wine. Rest you merry!

Exit.

BENVOLIO

At this same ancient feast of Capulet's
Sups the fair Rosaline whom thou so lov'st;
With all the admired beauties of Verona.
Go thither, and with unattainted eye
Compare her face with some that I shall show,
And I will make thee think thy swan a crow.

ROMEO

When the devout religion of mine eye
Maintains such falsehood, then turn tears to
    fires;
And these, who, often drown'd, could never die,
Transparent heretics, be burnt for liars!
One fairer than my love? The all-seeing sun
Ne'er saw her match since first the world begun.

BENVOLIO

Tut! you saw her fair, none else being by,
Herself pois'd with herself in either eye;

But in that crystal scales let there be weigh'd

Your lady's love against some other maid

That I will show you shining at this feast,

And she shall scant show well that now seems
   best.

   ROMEO

I'll go along, no such sight to be shown,

But to rejoice in splendour of my own.

Exeunt.

SCENE III.

Capulet's *house.*

Enter Lady Capulet *and* Nurse.

Lady Capulet

Nurse, where's my daughter? Call her forth to me.

Nurse

Now, by my maidenhead at twelve year old,
I bade her come. What, lamb! what ladybird!
God forbid! Where's this girl? What, Juliet!

Enter Juliet.

Juliet

How now? Who calls?

NURSE
Your mother.

JULIET
Madam, I am here. What is your will?

LADY CAPULET
This is the matter. Nurse, give leave awhile,
We must talk in secret. Nurse, come back again;
I have rememb'red me, thou's hear our counsel.
Thou knowest my daughter's of a pretty age.

NURSE
Faith, I can tell her age unto an hour.

LADY CAPULET
She's not fourteen.

NURSE

I'll lay fourteen of my teeth—
And yet, to my teen be it spoken, I have but four—
She is not fourteen. How long is it now
To Lammastide?

LADY CAPULET

A fortnight and odd days.

NURSE

Even or odd, of all days in the year,
Come Lammas Eve at night shall she be fourteen.
Susan and she (God rest all Christian souls!)
Were of an age. Well, Susan is with God;
She was too good for me. But, as I said,
On Lammas Eve at night shall she be fourteen;
That shall she, marry; I remember it well.
'Tis since the earthquake now eleven years;
And she was wean'd (I never shall forget it),
Of all the days of the year, upon that day;

For I had then laid wormwood to my dug,

Sitting in the sun under the dovehouse wall.

My lord and you were then at Mantua.

Nay, I do bear a brain. But, as I said,

When it did taste the wormwood on the nipple

Of my dug and felt it bitter, pretty fool,

To see it tetchy and fall out with the dug!

Shake, quoth the dovehouse! 'Twas no need, I
    trow,

To bid me trudge.

And since that time it is eleven years,

For then she could stand high-lone; nay, by th'
    rood,

She could have run and waddled all about;

For even the day before, she broke her brow;

And then my husband (God be with his soul!

'A was a merry man) took up the child.

"Yea," quoth he, "dost thou fall upon thy face?

Thou wilt fall backward when thou hast more
    wit;

Wilt thou not, Jule?" and, by my holidam,

The pretty wretch left crying, and said "Ay."

To see now how a jest shall come about!
I warrant, an I should live a thousand years,
I never should forget it. "Wilt thou not, Jule?"
    quoth he,
And, pretty fool, it stinted, and said "Ay."

LADY CAPULET

Enough of this. I pray thee hold thy peace.

NURSE

Yes, madam. Yet I cannot choose but laugh
To think it should leave crying and say "Ay."
And yet, I warrant, it had upon its brow
A bump as big as a young cock'rel's stone;
A perilous knock; and it cried bitterly.
"Yea," quoth my husband, "fall'st upon thy face?
Thou wilt fall backward when thou comest to
    age;
Wilt thou not, Jule?" It stinted, and said "Ay."

JULIET

And stint thou too, I pray thee, Nurse, say I.

NURSE

Peace, I have done. God mark thee to his grace!
Thou wast the prettiest babe that e'er I nurs'd.
An I might live to see thee married once,
I have my wish.

LADY CAPULET

Marry, that "marry" is the very theme
I came to talk of. Tell me, daughter Juliet,
How stands your disposition to be married?

JULIET

It is an honour that I dream not of.

NURSE

An honour? Were not I thine only nurse,

I would say thou hadst suck'd wisdom from thy

    teat.

LADY CAPULET

Well, think of marriage now. Younger than you,

Here in Verona, ladies of esteem,

Are made already mothers. By my count,

I was your mother much upon these years

That you are now a maid. Thus then in brief:

The valiant Paris seeks you for his love.

NURSE

A man, young lady! lady, such a man

As all the world—why he's a man of wax.

LADY CAPULET

Verona's summer hath not such a flower.

NURSE

Nay, he's a flower, in faith—a very flower.

LADY CAPULET

What say you? Can you love the gentleman?

This night you shall behold him at our feast.

Read o'er the volume of young Paris' face,

And find delight writ there with beauty's pen;

Examine every married lineament,

And see how one another lends content;

And what obscur'd in this fair volume lies

Find written in the margent of his eyes,

This precious book of love, this unbound lover,

To beautify him only lacks a cover.

The fish lives in the sea, and 'tis much pride

For fair without the fair within to hide.

That book in many's eyes doth share the glory,

That in gold clasps locks in the golden story;

So shall you share all that he doth possess,

By having him making yourself no less.

NURSE

No less? Nay, bigger! Women grow by men.

LADY CAPULET

Speak briefly, can you like of Paris' love?

JULIET

I'll look to like, if looking liking move;
But no more deep will I endart mine eye
Than your consent gives strength to make it fly.

Enter SERVINGMAN.

SERVINGMAN

Madam, the guests are come, supper serv'd up,
you call'd, my young lady ask'd for, the nurse
curs'd in the pantry, and everything in extremity.
I must hence to wait. I beseech you follow
straight.

LADY CAPULET
We follow thee.

Exit SERVINGMAN.

Juliet, the County stays.

NURSE
Go, girl, seek happy nights to happy days.

Exeunt.

SCENE IV.

A street.

Enter ROMEO, MERCUTIO, BENVOLIO, *with five or six other* MASKERS *and* TORCHBEARERS.

ROMEO

What, shall this speech be spoke for our
    excuse?
Or shall we on without apology?

BENVOLIO

The date is out of such prolixity.
We'll have no Cupid hoodwink'd with a scarf,
Bearing a Tartar's painted bow of lath,
Scaring the ladies like a crowkeeper;
Nor no without-book prologue, faintly spoke
After the prompter, for our entrance;
But, let them measure us by what they will,
We'll measure them a measure, and be gone.

ROMEO

Give me a torch. I am not for this ambling.

Being but heavy, I will bear the light.

MERCUTIO

Nay, gentle Romeo, we must have you dance.

ROMEO

Not I, believe me. You have dancing shoes

With nimble soles; I have a soul of lead

So stakes me to the ground I cannot move.

MERCUTIO

You are a lover. Borrow Cupid's wings

And soar with them above a common bound.

ROMEO

I am too sore enpierced with his shaft

To soar with his light feathers; and so bound
I cannot bound a pitch above dull woe.
Under love's heavy burthen do I sink.

MERCUTIO

And, to sink in it, should you burthen love—
Too great oppression for a tender thing.

ROMEO

Is love a tender thing? It is too rough,
Too rude, too boist'rous, and it pricks like thorn.

MERCUTIO

If love be rough with you, be rough with love.
Prick love for pricking, and you beat love down.
Give me a case to put my visage in.
A visor for a visor! What care I
What curious eye doth quote deformities?
Here are the beetle brows shall blush for me.

BENVOLIO

Come, knock and enter; and no sooner in
But every man betake him to his legs.

ROMEO

A torch for me! Let wantons light of heart
Tickle the senseless rushes with their heels;
For I am proverb'd with a grandsire phrase,
I'll be a candle-holder and look on;
The game was ne'er so fair, and I am done.

MERCUTIO

Tut! dun's the mouse, the constable's own word!
If thou art dun, we'll draw thee from the mire
Of this sir-reverence love, wherein thou stick'st
Up to the ears. Come, we burn daylight, ho!

ROMEO

Nay, that's not so.

MERCUTIO

I mean, sir, in delay
We waste our lights in vain, like lamps by day.
Take our good meaning, for our judgment sits
Five times in that ere once in our five wits.

ROMEO

And we mean well, in going to this masque;
But 'tis no wit to go.

MERCUTIO

Why, may one ask?

ROMEO

I dreamt a dream to-night.

MERCUTIO

And so did I.

ROMEO

Well, what was yours?

MERCUTIO

That dreamers often lie.

ROMEO

In bed asleep, while they do dream things true.

MERCUTIO

O, then I see Queen Mab hath been with you.
She is the fairies' midwife, and she comes
In shape no bigger than an agate stone
On the forefinger of an alderman,
Drawn with a team of little atomies
Athwart men's noses as they lie asleep;
Her wagon spokes made of long spinners' legs,
The cover, of the wings of grasshoppers;
Her traces, of the smallest spider's web;

Her collars, of the moonshine's wat'ry beams;

Her whip, of cricket's bone; the lash, of film;

Her wagoner, a small grey-coated gnat,

Not half so big as a round little worm

Prick'd from the lazy finger of a maid;

Her chariot is an empty hazelnut,

Made by the joiner squirrel or old grub,

Time out o' mind the fairies' coachmakers.

And in this state she gallops night by night

Through lovers' brains, and then they dream of
　　love;

O'er courtiers' knees, that dream on cursies
　　straight;

O'er lawyers' fingers, who straight dream on
　　fees;

O'er ladies' lips, who straight on kisses dream,

Which oft the angry Mab with blisters plagues,

Because their breaths with sweetmeats tainted
　　are.

Sometime she gallops o'er a courtier's nose,

And then dreams he of smelling out a suit;

And sometime comes she with a tithe-pig's tail

Tickling a parson's nose as 'a lies asleep,
Then dreams he of another benefice.
Sometimes she driveth o'er a soldier's neck,
And then dreams he of cutting foreign throats,
Of breaches, ambuscadoes, Spanish blades,
Of healths five fathoms deep; and then anon
Drums in his ear, at which he starts and wakes,
And being thus frighted, swears a prayer or two
And sleeps again. This is that very Mab
That plats the manes of horses in the night
And bakes the elflocks in foul sluttish hairs,
Which once untangled much misfortune bodes.
This is the hag, when maids lie on their backs,
That presses them and learns them first to bear,
Making them women of good carriage.
This is she—

ROMEO
Peace, peace, Mercutio, peace!
Thou talk'st of nothing.

MERCUTIO

True, I talk of dreams;

Which are the children of an idle brain,

Begot of nothing but vain fantasy;

Which is as thin of substance as the air,

And more inconstant than the wind, who wooes

Even now the frozen bosom of the North

And, being anger'd, puffs away from thence,

Turning his face to the dew-dropping South.

BENVOLIO

This wind you talk of blows us from ourselves.

Supper is done, and we shall come too late.

ROMEO

I fear, too early; for my mind misgives

Some consequence, yet hanging in the stars,

Shall bitterly begin his fearful date

With this night's revels and expire the term

Of a despised life, clos'd in my breast,

By some vile forfeit of untimely death.

But he that hath the steerage of my course

Direct my sail! On, lusty gentlemen!

BENVOLIO

Strike, drum. *[They march about the stage.]*

Exeunt.

SCENE V.

CAPULET'S *house.*

SERVINGMEN *come forth with napkins.*

FIRST SERVINGMAN

Where's Potpan, that he helps not to take away?
He shift a trencher! he scrape a trencher!

SECOND SERVINGMAN

When good manners shall lie all in one or two
men's hands, and they unwash'd too, 'tis a foul
thing.

FIRST SERVINGMAN

Away with the join-stools, remove the court-
cubbert, look to the plate. Good thou, save me
a piece of marchpane and, as thou loves me,

let the porter let in Susan Grindstone and Nell.
Anthony, and Potpan!

Second Servingman
Ay, boy, ready.

First Servingman
You are look'd for and call'd for, ask'd for and
sought for, in the great chamber.

Third Servingman
We cannot be here and there too. Cheerly, boys!
Be brisk awhile, and the longer liver take all.

Exeunt.

Enter the Maskers, Servants, Capulet, Lady Capulet,
Juliet, Tybalt, *and all the* Guests *and* Gentlewomen *to
the* Maskers.

CAPULET

Welcome, gentlemen! Ladies that have their toes

Unplagu'd with corns will have a bout with you.

Ah ha, my mistresses! which of you all

Will now deny to dance? She that makes dainty,

She I'll swear hath corns. Am I come near ye now?

Welcome, gentlemen! I have seen the day

That I have worn a visor and could tell

A whispering tale in a fair lady's ear,

Such as would please. 'Tis gone, 'tis gone, 'tis gone!

You are welcome, gentlemen! Come, musicians,
    play.

A hall, a hall! give room! and foot it, girls.

[Music plays, and they dance.]

More light, you knaves! and turn the tables up,

And quench the fire, the room is grown too hot.

Ah, sirrah, this unlook'd-for sport comes well.

Nay, sit, nay, sit, good cousin Capulet,

For you and I are past our dancing days.

How long is't now since last yourself and I

Were in a mask?

SECOND CAPULET

By'r Lady, thirty years.

CAPULET

What, man? 'Tis not so much, 'tis not so much!
'Tis since the nuptial of Lucentio,
Come Pentecost as quickly as it will,
Some five-and-twenty years, and then we
     mask'd.

SECOND CAPULET

'Tis more, 'tis more! His son is elder, sir;
His son is thirty.

CAPULET

Will you tell me that?
His son was but a ward two years ago.

ROMEO

[to a SERVINGMAN*]* What lady's that, which doth
    enrich the hand
Of yonder knight?

SERVINGMAN

I know not, sir.

ROMEO

O, she doth teach the torches to burn bright!
It seems she hangs upon the cheek of night
Like a rich jewel in an Ethiop's ear—
Beauty too rich for use, for earth too dear!
So shows a snowy dove trooping with crows
As yonder lady o'er her fellows shows.
The measure done, I'll watch her place of stand
And, touching hers, make blessed my rude hand.
Did my heart love till now? Forswear it, sight!
For I ne'er saw true beauty till this night.

TYBALT

This, by his voice, should be a Montague.
Fetch me my rapier, boy. What, dares the slave
Come hither, cover'd with an antic face,
To fleer and scorn at our solemnity?
Now, by the stock and honour of my kin,
To strike him dead I hold it not a sin.

CAPULET

Why, how now, kinsman? Wherefore storm you
    so?

TYBALT

Uncle, this is a Montague, our foe;
A villain, that is hither come in spite
To scorn at our solemnity this night.

CAPULET

Young Romeo is it?

TYBALT

'Tis he, that villain Romeo.

CAPULET

Content thee, gentle coz, let him alone.
'A bears him like a portly gentleman,
And, to say truth, Verona brags of him
To be a virtuous and well-govern'd youth.
I would not for the wealth of all this town
Here in my house do him disparagement.
Therefore be patient, take no note of him.
It is my will; the which if thou respect,
Show a fair presence and put off these frowns,
An ill-beseeming semblance for a feast.

TYBALT

It fits when such a villain is a guest.
I'll not endure him.

CAPULET

He shall be endur'd.

What, goodman boy? I say he shall. Go to!

Am I the master here, or you? Go to!

You'll not endure him? God shall mend my soul!

You'll make a mutiny among my guests!

You will set cock-a-hoop! you'll be the man!

TYBALT

Why, uncle, 'tis a shame.

CAPULET

Go to, go to!

You are a saucy boy. Is't so, indeed?

This trick may chance to scathe you. I know
    what.

You must contrary me! Marry, 'tis time.—

Well said, my hearts!—You are a princox—go!

Be quiet, or—More light, more light!—For shame!

I'll make you quiet; what!—Cheerly, my hearts!

TYBALT

Patience perforce with wilful choler meeting
Makes my flesh tremble in their different
  greeting.
I will withdraw; but this intrusion shall,
Now seeming sweet, convert to bitt'rest gall.

Exit.

ROMEO

[to JULIET*]* If I profane with my unworthiest hand
This holy shrine, the gentle fine is this:
My lips, two blushing pilgrims, ready stand
To smooth that rough touch with a tender kiss.

JULIET

Good pilgrim, you do wrong your hand too much,
Which mannerly devotion shows in this;
For saints have hands that pilgrims' hands do
  touch,
And palm to palm is holy palmers' kiss.

ROMEO

Have not saints lips, and holy palmers too?

JULIET

Ay, pilgrim, lips that they must use in pray'r.

ROMEO

O, then, dear saint, let lips do what hands do!
They pray; grant thou, lest faith turn to despair.

JULIET

Saints do not move, though grant for prayers'
    sake.

ROMEO

Then move not while my prayer's effect I take.
Thus from my lips, by thine my sin is purg'd

[Kisses her.]

JULIET

Then have my lips the sin that they have took.

ROMEO

Sin from my lips? O trespass sweetly urg'd!
Give me my sin again. *[Kisses her.]*

JULIET

You kiss by th' book.

NURSE

Madam, your mother craves a word with you.

ROMEO

What is her mother?

Nurse

Marry, bachelor,

Her mother is the lady of the house.

And a good lady, and a wise and virtuous.

I nurs'd her daughter that you talk'd withal.

I tell you, he that can lay hold of her

Shall have the chinks.

Romeo

Is she a Capulet?

O dear account! my life is my foe's debt.

Benvolio

Away, be gone; the sport is at the best.

Romeo

Ay, so I fear; the more is my unrest.

CAPULET

Nay, gentlemen, prepare not to be gone;

We have a trifling foolish banquet towards.

Is it e'en so? Why then, I thank you all.

I thank you, honest gentlemen. Good night.

More torches here! Come on then, let's to bed.

Ah, sirrah, by my fay, it waxes late;

I'll to my rest.

Exeunt all but JULIET *and* NURSE.

JULIET

Come hither, Nurse. What is yond gentleman?

NURSE

The son and heir of old Tiberio.

JULIET

What's he that now is going out of door?

NURSE
Marry, that, I think, be young Petruchio.

JULIET
What's he that follows there, that would not
dance?

NURSE
I know not.

JULIET
Go ask his name.—If he be married,
My grave is like to be my wedding bed.

NURSE
His name is Romeo, and a Montague,
The only son of your great enemy.

JULIET

My only love, sprung from my only hate!
Too early seen unknown, and known too late!
Prodigious birth of love it is to me
That I must love a loathed enemy.

NURSE

What's this? what's this?

JULIET

A rhyme I learnt even now
Of one I danc'd withal.

[One calls within, "Juliet."]

NURSE

Anon, anon!
Come, let's away; the strangers all are gone.

Exeunt.

ACT II.

PROLOGUE

Enter Chorus.

Chorus

Now old desire doth in his deathbed lie,
And young affection gapes to be his heir;
That fair for which love groan'd for and would die,
With tender Juliet match'd, is now not fair.
Now Romeo is belov'd, and loves again,
Alike bewitched by the charm of looks;
But to his foe suppos'd he must complain,
And she steal love's sweet bait from fearful hooks.
Being held a foe, he may not have access
To breathe such vows as lovers use to swear,
And she as much in love, her means much less
To meet her new beloved anywhere;
But passion lends them power, time means, to
    meet,
Temp'ring extremities with extreme sweet.

Exit.

ACT II.

SCENE I.

A lane by the wall of CAPULET's *orchard.*

Enter ROMEO *alone.*

ROMEO
Can I go forward when my heart is here?
Turn back, dull earth, and find thy centre out.
[He climbs the wall and leaps down within it.]

Enter BENVOLIO *with* MERCUTIO.

BENVOLIO
Romeo! my cousin Romeo! Romeo!

MERCUTIO
He is wise,
And, on my life, hath stol'n him home to bed.

BENVOLIO

He ran this way, and leapt this orchard wall.
Call, good Mercutio.

MERCUTIO

Nay, I'll conjure too.
Romeo! humours! madman! passion! lover!
Appear thou in the likeness of a sigh;
Speak but one rhyme, and I am satisfied!
Cry but "Ay me!" pronounce but "love" and
    "dove";
Speak to my gossip Venus one fair word,
One nickname for her purblind son and heir,
Young Adam Cupid, he that shot so trim
When King Cophetua lov'd the beggar maid!
He heareth not, he stirreth not, be moveth not;
The ape is dead, and I must conjure him.
I conjure thee by Rosaline's bright eyes.
By her high forehead and her scarlet lip,
By her fine foot, straight leg, and quivering thigh,

And the demesnes that there adjacent lie,
That in thy likeness thou appear to us!

BENVOLIO
An if he hear thee, thou wilt anger him.

MERCUTIO
This cannot anger him. 'Twould anger him
To raise a spirit in his mistress' circle
Of some strange nature, letting it there stand
Till she had laid it and conjur'd it down.
That were some spite; my invocation
Is fair and honest: in his mistress' name,
I conjure only but to raise up him.

BENVOLIO
Come, he hath hid himself among these trees
To be consorted with the humorous night.
Blind is his love and best befits the dark.

MERCUTIO
If love be blind, love cannot hit the mark.
Now will he sit under a medlar tree
And wish his mistress were that kind of fruit
As maids call medlars when they laugh alone.
O, Romeo, that she were, O that she were
An open et cetera, thou a pop'rin pear!
Romeo, good night. I'll to my truckle-bed;
This field-bed is too cold for me to sleep.
Come, shall we go?

BENVOLIO
Go then, for 'tis in vain
To seek him here that means not to be found.

Exeunt.

SCENE II.
CAPULET'*s orchard.*

Enter ROMEO.

ROMEO

He jests at scars that never felt a wound.

Enter JULIET *above at a window.*

But soft! What light through yonder window
    breaks?
It is the East, and Juliet is the sun!
Arise, fair sun, and kill the envious moon,
Who is already sick and pale with grief
That thou her maid art far more fair than she.
Be not her maid, since she is envious.
Her vestal livery is but sick and green,
And none but fools do wear it. Cast it off.
It is my lady; O, it is my love!
O that she knew she were!

She speaks, yet she says nothing. What of
that?
Her eye discourses; I will answer it.
I am too bold; 'tis not to me she speaks.
Two of the fairest stars in all the heaven,
Having some business, do entreat her eyes
To twinkle in their spheres till they return.
What if her eyes were there, they in her head?
The brightness of her cheek would shame those
stars
As daylight doth a lamp; her eyes in heaven
Would through the airy region stream so bright
That birds would sing and think it were not
night.
See how she leans her cheek upon her hand!
O that I were a glove upon that hand,
That I might touch that cheek!

JULIET
Ay me!

ROMEO

She speaks.

O, speak again, bright angel! for thou art

As glorious to this night, being o'er my head,

As is a winged messenger of heaven

Unto the white-upturned wond'ring eyes

Of mortals that fall back to gaze on him

When he bestrides the lazy-pacing clouds

And sails upon the bosom of the air.

JULIET

O Romeo, Romeo! wherefore art thou Romeo?

Deny thy father and refuse thy name!

Or, if thou wilt not, be but sworn my love,

And I'll no longer be a Capulet.

ROMEO

[aside] Shall I hear more, or shall I speak at

this?

JULIET

'Tis but thy name that is my enemy.

Thou art thyself, though not a Montague.

What's Montague? it is nor hand, nor foot,

Nor arm, nor face, nor any other part

Belonging to a man. O, be some other name!

What's in a name? That which we call a rose

By any other name would smell as sweet.

So Romeo would, were he not Romeo call'd,

Retain that dear perfection which he owes

Without that title. Romeo, doff thy name;

And for that name, which is no part of thee,

Take all myself.

ROMEO

I take thee at thy word.

Call me but love, and I'll be new baptiz'd;

Henceforth I never will be Romeo.

JULIET

What man art thou that, thus bescreen'd in
　　night,
So stumblest on my counsel?

ROMEO

By a name
I know not how to tell thee who I am.
My name, dear saint, is hateful to myself,
Because it is an enemy to thee.
Had I it written, I would tear the word.

JULIET

My ears have yet not drunk a hundred words
Of that tongue's utterance, yet I know the sound.
Art thou not Romeo, and a Montague?

ROMEO

Neither, fair saint, if either thee dislike.

JULIET

How cam'st thou hither, tell me, and wherefore?

The orchard walls are high and hard to climb,

And the place death, considering who thou art,

If any of my kinsmen find thee here.

ROMEO

With love's light wings did I o'erperch these walls;

For stony limits cannot hold love out,

And what love can do, that dares love attempt.

Therefore thy kinsmen are no let to me.

JULIET

If they do see thee, they will murder thee.

ROMEO

Alack, there lies more peril in thine eye

Than twenty of their swords! Look thou but sweet,

And I am proof against their enmity.

JULIET

I would not for the world they saw thee here.

ROMEO

I have night's cloak to hide me from their sight;
And but thou love me, let them find me here.
My life were better ended by their hate
Than death prorogued, wanting of thy love.

JULIET

By whose direction found'st thou out this place?

ROMEO

By love, that first did prompt me to enquire.
He lent me counsel, and I lent him eyes.
I am no pilot; yet, wert thou as far
As that vast shore wash'd with the farthest sea,
I would adventure for such merchandise.

JULIET

Thou knowest the mask of night is on my face;

Else would a maiden blush bepaint my cheek

For that which thou hast heard me speak

    to-night.

Fain would I dwell on form—fain, fain deny

What I have spoke; but farewell compliment!

Dost thou love me, I know thou wilt say "Ay";

And I will take thy word. Yet, if thou swear'st,

Thou mayst prove false. At lovers' perjuries,

They say Jove laughs. O gentle Romeo,

If thou dost love, pronounce it faithfully.

Or if thou thinkest I am too quickly won,

I'll frown, and be perverse, and say thee nay,

So thou wilt woo; but else, not for the world.

In truth, fair Montague, I am too fond,

And therefore thou mayst think my 'haviour light;

But trust me, gentleman, I'll prove more true

Than those that have more cunning to be strange.

I should have been more strange, I must confess,

But that thou overheard'st, ere I was ware,

My true-love passion. Therefore pardon me,

And not impute this yielding to light love,
Which the dark night hath so discovered.

ROMEO
Lady, by yonder blessed moon I swear,
That tips with silver all these fruit-tree tops—

JULIET
O, swear not by the moon, th' inconstant moon,
That monthly changes in her circled orb,
Lest that thy love prove likewise variable.

ROMEO
What shall I swear by?

JULIET
Do not swear at all;
Or if thou wilt, swear by thy gracious self,

Which is the god of my idolatry,
And I'll believe thee.

ROMEO
If my heart's dear love—

JULIET
Well, do not swear. Although I joy in thee,
I have no joy of this contract to-night.
It is too rash, too unadvis'd, too sudden;
Too like the lightning, which doth cease to be
Ere one can say "It lightens." Sweet, good night!
This bud of love, by summer's ripening breath,
May prove a beauteous flow'r when next we meet.
Good night, good night! As sweet repose and rest
Come to thy heart as that within my breast!

ROMEO
O, wilt thou leave me so unsatisfied?

JULIET

What satisfaction canst thou have to-night?

ROMEO

Th' exchange of thy love's faithful vow for mine.

JULIET

I gave thee mine before thou didst request it;
And yet I would it were to give again.

ROMEO

Would'st thou withdraw it? For what purpose,
   love?

JULIET

But to be frank and give it thee again.
And yet I wish but for the thing I have.
My bounty is as boundless as the sea,

My love as deep; the more I give to thee,

The more I have, for both are infinite.

I hear some noise within. Dear love, adieu!

*[*Nurse *calls within.]*

Anon, good nurse! Sweet Montague, be true.

Stay but a little, I will come again.

Exit.

Romeo

O blessed, blessed night! I am afeard,

Being in night, all this is but a dream,

Too flattering-sweet to be substantial.

Enter Juliet *above.*

Juliet

Three words, dear Romeo, and good night
   indeed.

If that thy bent of love be honourable,

Thy purpose marriage, send me word to-morrow,

By one that I'll procure to come to thee,

Where and what time thou wilt perform the
       rite;

And all my fortunes at thy foot I'll lay

And follow thee my lord throughout the world.

NURSE

[within] **Madam!**

JULIET

I come, anon.—But if thou meanest not well,

I do beseech thee—

NURSE

[within] **Madam!**

JULIET

By-and-by I come.—

To cease thy suit and leave me to my grief.
To-morrow will I send.

ROMEO
So thrive my soul—

JULIET
A thousand times good night!

Exit.

ROMEO
A thousand times the worse, to want thy light!
Love goes toward love as schoolboys from their
  books;
But love from love, toward school with heavy
  looks.

Enter JULIET *again, above.*

JULIET

Hist! Romeo, hist! O for a falconer's voice
To lure this tassel-gentle back again!
Bondage is hoarse and may not speak aloud;
Else would I tear the cave where Echo lies,
And make her airy tongue more hoarse than mine
With repetition of my Romeo's name.
Romeo!

ROMEO

It is my soul that calls upon my name.
How silver-sweet sound lovers' tongues by night,
Like softest music to attending ears!

JULIET

Romeo!

ROMEO

My dear?

JULIET

At what o'clock to-morrow
Shall I send to thee?

ROMEO

By the hour of nine.

JULIET

I will not fail. 'Tis twenty years till then.
I have forgot why I did call thee back.

ROMEO

Let me stand here till thou remember it.

JULIET

I shall forget, to have thee still stand there,
Rememb'ring how I love thy company.

ROMEO

And I'll still stay, to have thee still forget,
Forgetting any other home but this.

JULIET

'Tis almost morning. I would have thee gone—
And yet no farther than a wanton's bird,
That lets it hop a little from her hand,
Like a poor prisoner in his twisted gyves,
And with a silk thread plucks it back again,
So loving-jealous of his liberty.

ROMEO

I would I were thy bird.

JULIET

Sweet, so would I.
Yet I should kill thee with much cherishing.

Good night, good night! Parting is such sweet
sorrow,
That I shall say good night till it be morrow.

Exit.

ROMEO
Sleep dwell upon thine eyes, peace in thy breast!
Would I were sleep and peace, so sweet to rest!
Hence will I to my ghostly father's cell,
His help to crave and my dear hap to tell.

Exit.

SCENE III.

Enter FRIAR LAURENCE *alone, with a basket.*

FRIAR LAURENCE

The grey-ey'd morn smiles on the frowning
    night,
Check'ring the Eastern clouds with streaks of
    light;
And flecked darkness like a drunkard reels
From forth day's path and Titan's fiery wheels.
Non, ere the sun advance his burning eye
The day to cheer and night's dank dew to dry,
I must up-fill this osier cage of ours
With baleful weeds and precious-juiced flowers.
The earth that's nature's mother is her tomb.
What is her burying grave, that is her womb;
And from her womb children of divers kind
We sucking on her natural bosom find;
Many for many virtues excellent,

None but for some, and yet all different.

O, mickle is the powerful grace that lies

In plants, herbs, stones, and their true qualities;

For naught so vile that on the earth doth live

But to the earth some special good doth give;

Nor aught so good but, strain'd from that fair
     use,

Revolts from true birth, stumbling on abuse.

Virtue itself turns vice, being misapplied,

And vice sometime by action dignified.

Within the infant rind of this small flower

Poison hath residence, and medicine power;

For this, being smelt, with that part cheers each
     part;

Being tasted, slays all senses with the heart.

Two such opposed kings encamp them still

In man as well as herbs—grace and rude will;

And where the worser is predominant,

Full soon the canker death eats up that plant.

Enter ROMEO.

ROMEO

Good morrow, father.

FRIAR LAURENCE

Benedicite!

What early tongue so sweet saluteth me?

Young son, it argues a distempered head

So soon to bid good morrow to thy bed.

Care keeps his watch in every old man's eye,

And where care lodges sleep will never lie;

But where unbruised youth with unstuff'd brain

Doth couch his limbs, there golden sleep doth
    reign.

Therefore thy earliness doth me assure

Thou art uprous'd with some distemp'rature;

Or if not so, then here I hit it right—

Our Romeo hath not been in bed to-night.

ROMEO

That last is true—the sweeter rest was mine.

FRIAR LAURENCE

God pardon sin! Wast thou with Rosaline?

ROMEO

With Rosaline, my ghostly father? No.

I have forgot that name, and that name's woe.

FRIAR LAURENCE

That's my good son! But where hast thou been
then?

ROMEO

I'll tell thee ere thou ask it me again.

I have been feasting with mine enemy,

Where on a sudden one hath wounded me

That's by me wounded. Both our remedies

Within thy help and holy physic lies.

I bear no hatred, blessed man, for, lo,

My intercession likewise steads my foe.

Friar Laurence

Be plain, good son, and homely in thy drift.
Riddling confession finds but riddling shrift.

Romeo

Then plainly know my heart's dear love is set
On the fair daughter of rich Capulet;
As mine on hers, so hers is set on mine,
And all combin'd, save what thou must combine
By holy marriage. When, and where, and how
We met, we woo'd, and made exchange of vow,
I'll tell thee as we pass; but this I pray,
That thou consent to marry us to-day.

Friar Laurence

Holy Saint Francis! What a change is here!
Is Rosaline, that thou didst love so dear,
So soon forsaken? Young men's love then lies
Not truly in their hearts, but in their eyes.
Jesu Maria! What a deal of brine

Hath wash'd thy sallow cheeks for Rosaline!

How much salt water thrown away in waste,

To season love, that of it doth not taste!

The sun not yet thy sighs from heaven clears,

Thy old groans ring yet in mine ancient ears.

Lo, here upon thy cheek the stain doth sit

Of an old tear that is not wash'd off yet.

If e'er thou wast thyself, and these woes thine,

Thou and these woes were all for Rosaline.

And art thou chang'd? Pronounce this sentence
then:

Women may fall when there's no strength in
men.

ROMEO

Thou chid'st me oft for loving Rosaline.

FRIAR LAURENCE

For doting, not for loving, pupil mine.

ROMEO

And bad'st me bury love.

FRIAR LAURENCE

Not in a grave
To lay one in, another out to have.

ROMEO

I pray thee chide not. She whom I love now
Doth grace for grace and love for love allow.
The other did not so.

FRIAR LAURENCE

O, she knew well
Thy love did read by rote, that could not spell.
But come, young waverer, come go with me.
In one respect I'll thy assistant be;
For this alliance may so happy prove
To turn your households' rancour to pure love.

ROMEO

O, let us hence! I stand on sudden haste.

FRIAR LAURENCE

Wisely, and slow. They stumble that run fast.

Exeunt.

SCENE IV.

A street.

Enter BENVOLIO *and* MERCUTIO.

MERCUTIO

Where the devil should this Romeo be?
Came he not home to-night?

BENVOLIO

Not to his father's. I spoke with his man.

MERCUTIO

Why, that same pale hard-hearted wench, that
   Rosaline,
Torments him so that he will sure run mad.

BENVOLIO

Tybalt, the kinsman to old Capulet,

Hath sent a letter to his father's house.

MERCUTIO

A challenge, on my life.

BENVOLIO

Romeo will answer it.

MERCUTIO

Any man that can write may answer a letter.

BENVOLIO

Nay, he will answer the letter's master, how he
dares, being dared.

MERCUTIO

Alas, poor Romeo, he is already dead! stabb'd
with a white wench's black eye; shot through the
ear with a love song; the very pin of his heart
cleft with the blind bow-boy's butt-shaft; and is
he a man to encounter Tybalt?

BENVOLIO

Why, what is Tybalt?

MERCUTIO

More than Prince of Cats, I can tell you. O,
he's the courageous captain of compliments.
He fights as you sing pricksong—keeps time,
distance, and proportion; rests me his minim
rest, one, two, and the third in your bosom!
the very butcher of a silk button, a duellist, a
duellist! a gentleman of the very first house, of
the first and second cause. Ah, the immortal
passado! the punto reverse! the hay.

BENVOLIO

The what?

MERCUTIO

The pox of such antic, lisping, affecting
fantasticoes—these new tuners of accent!
"By Jesu, a very good blade! a very tall man!
a very good whore!" Why, is not this a
lamentable thing, grandsir, that we should be
thus afflicted with these strange flies, these
fashion-mongers, these pardona-mi's, who stand
so much on the new form that they cannot sit
at ease on the old bench? O, their bones, their
bones!

Enter ROMEO.

BENVOLIO

Here comes Romeo! here comes Romeo!

MERCUTIO

Without his roe, like a dried herring. O flesh, flesh, how art thou fishified! Now is he for the numbers that Petrarch flowed in. Laura, to his lady, was but a kitchen wench (marry, she had a better love to berhyme her), Dido a dowdy, Cleopatra a gypsy, Helen and Hero hildings and harlots, Thisbe a grey eye or so, but not to the purpose. Signior Romeo, bon jour! There's a French salutation to your French slop. You gave us the counterfeit fairly last night.

ROMEO

Good morrow to you both. What counterfeit did I give you?

MERCUTIO

The slip, sir, the slip. Can you not conceive?

ROMEO

Pardon, good Mercutio. My business was great, and in such a case as mine a man may strain courtesy.

MERCUTIO

That's as much as to say, such a case as yours constrains a man to bow in the hams.

ROMEO

Meaning, to curtsy.

MERCUTIO

Thou hast most kindly hit it.

ROMEO

A most courteous exposition.

MERCUTIO

Nay, I am the very pink of courtesy.

ROMEO

Pink for flower.

MERCUTIO

Right.

ROMEO

Why, then is my pump well-flower'd.

MERCUTIO

Well said! Follow me this jest now till thou hast
worn out thy pump, that, when the single sole
of it is worn, the jest may remain, after the
wearing, solely singular.

ROMEO

O single-soled jest, solely singular for the
singleness!

MERCUTIO

Come between us, good Benvolio! My wits
faint.

ROMEO

Swits and spurs, swits and spurs! or I'll cry a
match.

MERCUTIO

Nay, if our wits run the wild-goose chase, I
am done; for thou hast more of the wild goose
in one of thy wits than, I am sure, I have in
my whole five. Was I with you there for the
goose?

ROMEO

Thou wast never with me for anything when
thou wast not there for the goose.

MERCUTIO

I will bite thee by the ear for that jest.

ROMEO

Nay, good goose, bite not!

MERCUTIO

Thy wit is a very bitter sweeting; it is a most
sharp sauce.

ROMEO

And is it not, then, well serv'd in to a sweet
goose?

MERCUTIO

O, here's a wit of cheveril, that stretches from an
inch narrow to an ell broad!

ROMEO

I stretch it out for that word "broad," which,
added to the goose, proves thee far and wide a
broad goose.

MERCUTIO

Why, is not this better now than groaning for
love? Now art thou sociable, now art thou
Romeo; now art thou what thou art, by art as
well as by nature. For this drivelling love is like
a great natural that runs lolling up and down to
hide his bauble in a hole.

BENVOLIO

Stop there, stop there!

MERCUTIO

Thou desirest me to stop in my tale against the
hair.

BENVOLIO

Thou wouldst else have made thy tale large.

MERCUTIO

O, thou art deceiv'd! I would have made it short;
for I was come to the whole depth of my tale,
and meant indeed to occupy the argument no
longer.

ROMEO

Here's goodly gear!

Enter NURSE *and her man,* PETER.

MERCUTIO
A sail, a sail!

BENVOLIO
Two, two! a shirt and a smock.

NURSE
Peter!

PETER
Anon.

NURSE
My fan, Peter.

MERCUTIO
Good Peter, to hide her face; for her fan's the
fairer face of the two.

NURSE

God ye good morrow, gentlemen.

MERCUTIO

God ye good-den, fair gentlewoman.

NURSE

Is it good-den?

MERCUTIO

'Tis no less, I tell ye; for the bawdy hand of the dial is now upon the prick of noon.

NURSE

Out upon you! What a man are you!

ROMEO

One, gentlewoman, that God hath made for
himself to mar.

NURSE

By my troth, it is well said. "For himself to mar,"
quoth 'a? Gentlemen, can any of you tell me
where I may find the young Romeo?

ROMEO

I can tell you; but young Romeo will be older
when you have found him than he was when
you sought him. I am the youngest of that name,
for fault of a worse.

NURSE

You say well.

MERCUTIO
Yea, is the worst well? Very well took, i' faith!
wisely, wisely.

NURSE
If you be he, sir, I desire some confidence with
you.

BENVOLIO
She will endite him to some supper.

MERCUTIO
A bawd, a bawd, a bawd! So ho!

ROMEO
What hast thou found?

MERCUTIO

No hare, sir; unless a hare, sir, in a lenten pie,
that is something stale and hoar ere it be spent.

[He walks by them and sings.]

> *An old hare hoar,*
> *And an old hare hoar,*
> *Is very good meat in Lent;*
> *But a hare that is hoar*
> *Is too much for a score*
> *When it hoars ere it be spent.*

Romeo, will you come to your father's? We'll to
dinner thither.

ROMEO

I will follow you.

MERCUTIO

Farewell, ancient lady. Farewell, *[sings]* lady, lady, lady.

Exeunt MERCUTIO *and* BENVOLIO.

NURSE

I pray you, Sir, what saucy merchant was this that was so full of his ropery?

ROMEO

A gentleman, Nurse, that loves to hear himself talk and will speak more in a minute than he will stand to in a month.

NURSE

An 'a speak anything against me, I'll take him down, an 'a were lustier than he is, and twenty such jacks; and if I cannot, I'll find those that

shall. Scurvy knave! I am none of his flirt-gills;
I am none of his skains-mates. And thou must
stand by too, and suffer every knave to use me at
his pleasure!

PETER

I saw no man use you at his pleasure. If I had,
my weapon should quickly have been out, I
warrant you. I dare draw as soon as another
man, if I see occasion in a good quarrel, and the
law on my side.

NURSE

Now, afore God, I am so vexed that every part
about me quivers. Scurvy knave! Pray you, sir,
a word; and, as I told you, my young lady bid
me enquire you out. What she bid me say, I
will keep to myself; but first let me tell ye, if ye
should lead her into a fool's paradise, as they
say, it were a very gross kind of behaviour, as

they say; for the gentlewoman is young; and
therefore, if you should deal double with her,
truly it were an ill thing to be off'red to any
gentlewoman, and very weak dealing.

Romeo

Nurse, commend me to thy lady and mistress. I
protest unto thee—

Nurse

Good heart, and i' faith I will tell her as much.
Lord, Lord! she will be a joyful woman.

Romeo

What wilt thou tell her, Nurse? Thou dost not
mark me.

NURSE

I will tell her, sir, that you do protest, which, as I take it, is a gentlemanlike offer.

ROMEO

Bid her devise
Some means to come to shrift this afternoon;
And there she shall at Friar Laurence's cell
Be shriv'd and married. Here is for thy pains.

NURSE

No, truly, sir; not a penny.

ROMEO

Go to! I say you shall.

NURSE

This afternoon, sir? Well, she shall be there.

ROMEO

And stay, good nurse, behind the abbey wall.

Within this hour my man shall be with thee

And bring thee cords made like a tackled stair,

Which to the high topgallant of my joy

Must be my convoy in the secret night.

Farewell. Be trusty, and I'll quit thy pains.

Farewell. Commend me to thy mistress.

NURSE

Now God in heaven bless thee! Hark you, sir.

ROMEO

What say'st thou, my dear nurse?

NURSE

Is your man secret? Did you ne'er hear say,

Two may keep counsel, putting one away?

ROMEO

I warrant thee my man's as true as steel.

NURSE

Well, sir, my mistress is the sweetest lady. Lord,
Lord! when 'twas a little prating thing—O, there
is a nobleman in town, one Paris, that would fain
lay knife aboard; but she, good soul, had as lieve
see a toad, a very toad, as see him. I anger her
sometimes, and tell her that Paris is the properer
man; but I'll warrant you, when I say so, she
looks as pale as any clout in the versal world.
Doth not rosemary and Romeo begin both with a
letter?

ROMEO

Ay, nurse; what of that? Both with an R.

NURSE

Ah, mocker! that's the dog's name. R is for the—

No; I know it begins with some other letter; and
she hath the prettiest sententious of it, of you and
rosemary, that it would do you good to hear it.

ROMEO
Commend me to thy lady.

NURSE
Ay, a thousand times.

Exit ROMEO.

Peter!

PETER
Anon.

NURSE
Peter, take my fan, and go before, and apace.

Exeunt.

SCENE V.

CAPULET'S *orchard.*

Enter JULIET.

JULIET

The clock struck nine when I did send the
    nurse;
In half an hour she promis'd to return.
Perchance she cannot meet him. That's not so.
O, she is lame! Love's heralds should be
    thoughts,
Which ten times faster glide than the sun's
    beams
Driving back shadows over low'ring hills.
Therefore do nimble-pinion'd doves draw Love,
And therefore hath the wind-swift Cupid wings.
Now is the sun upon the highmost hill
Of this day's journey, and from nine till twelve
Is three long hours; yet she is not come.
Had she affections and warm youthful blood,

She would be as swift in motion as a ball;
My words would bandy her to my sweet love,
And his to me,
But old folks, many feign as they were dead—
Unwieldy, slow, heavy and pale as lead.

Enter NURSE *and* PETER.

O God, she comes! O honey nurse, what news?
Hast thou met with him? Send thy man away.

NURSE
Peter, stay at the gate.

Exit PETER.

JULIET
Now, good sweet nurse—O Lord, why look'st
    thou sad?

Though news be sad, yet tell them merrily;
If good, thou shamest the music of sweet news
By playing it to me with so sour a face.

NURSE

I am aweary, give me leave awhile.
Fie, how my bones ache! What a jaunce have I
    had!

JULIET

I would thou hadst my bones, and I thy news.
Nay, come, I pray thee speak. Good, good nurse,
    speak.

NURSE

Jesu, what haste! Can you not stay awhile?
Do you not see that I am out of breath?

JULIET

How art thou out of breath when thou hast
    breath
To say to me that thou art out of breath?
The excuse that thou dost make in this delay
Is longer than the tale thou dost excuse.
Is thy news good or bad? Answer to that.
Say either, and I'll stay the circumstance.
Let me be satisfied, is't good or bad?

NURSE

Well, you have made a simple choice; you know
not how to choose a man. Romeo? No, not he.
Though his face be better than any man's, yet his
leg excels all men's; and for a hand and a foot,
and a body, though they be not to be talk'd on,
yet they are past compare. He is not the flower
of courtesy, but, I'll warrant him, as gentle as
a lamb. Go thy ways, wench; serve God. What,
have you din'd at home?

JULIET

No, no. But all this did I know before.

What says he of our marriage? What of that?

NURSE

Lord, how my head aches! What a head have I!

It beats as it would fall in twenty pieces.

My back o' t' other side,—ah, my back, my
   back!

Beshrew your heart for sending me about

To catch my death with jauncing up and down!

JULIET

I' faith, I am sorry that thou art not well.

Sweet, sweet, sweet nurse, tell me, what says my
   love?

NURSE

Your love says, like an honest gentleman, and

a courteous, and a kind, and a handsome;
and, I warrant, a virtuous—Where is your
mother?

JULIET
Where is my mother? Why, she is within.
Where should she be? How oddly thou repliest!
"Your love says, like an honest gentleman,
'Where is your mother?'"

NURSE
O God's Lady dear!
Are you so hot? Marry come up, I trow.
Is this the poultice for my aching bones?
Henceforward do your messages yourself.

JULIET
Here's such a coil! Come, what says Romeo?

NURSE

Have you got leave to go to shrift to-day?

JULIET

I have.

NURSE

Then hie you hence to Friar Laurence's cell;
There stays a husband to make you a wife.
Now comes the wanton blood up in your
    cheeks:
They'll be in scarlet straight at any news.
Hie you to church; I must another way,
To fetch a ladder, by the which your love
Must climb a bird's nest soon when it is dark.
I am the drudge, and toil in your delight;
But you shall bear the burthen soon at night.
Go; I'll to dinner; hie you to the cell.

JULIET
Hie to high fortune! Honest nurse, farewell.

Exeunt.

SCENE VI.

Enter FRIAR LAURENCE *and* ROMEO.

FRIAR LAURENCE

So smile the heavens upon this holy act
That after-hours with sorrow chide us not!

ROMEO

Amen, amen! But come what sorrow can,
It cannot countervail the exchange of joy
That one short minute gives me in her sight.
Do thou but close our hands with holy words,
Then love-devouring death do what he dare—
It is enough I may but call her mine.

FRIAR LAURENCE

These violent delights have violent ends

And in their triumph die, like fire and powder,
Which, as they kiss, consume. The sweetest
   honey
Is loathsome in his own deliciousness
And in the taste confounds the appetite.
Therefore love moderately: long love doth so;
Too swift arrives as tardy as too slow.

Enter JULIET.

Here comes the lady. O, so light a foot
Will ne'er wear out the everlasting flint.
A lover may bestride the gossamer
That idles in the wanton summer air,
And yet not fall; so light is vanity.

JULIET
Good even to my ghostly confessor.

FRIAR LAURENCE

Romeo shall thank thee, daughter, for us both.

JULIET

As much to him, else is his thanks too much.

ROMEO

Ah, Juliet, if the measure of thy joy
Be heap'd like mine, and that thy skill be more
To blazon it, then sweeten with thy breath
This neighbour air, and let rich music's tongue
Unfold the imagin'd happiness that both
Receive in either by this dear encounter.

JULIET

Conceit, more rich in matter than in words,
Brags of his substance, not of ornament.
They are but beggars that can count their
worth;

But my true love is grown to such excess
cannot sum up sum of half my wealth.

    FRIAR LAURENCE
Come, come with me, and we will make short
    work;
For, by your leaves, you shall not stay alone
Till Holy Church incorporate two in one.

Exeunt.

ACT III.

SCENE I.

A public place.

Enter MERCUTIO, BENVOLIO, *and* MEN.

BENVOLIO

I pray thee, good Mercutio, let's retire.
The day is hot, the Capulets abroad.
And if we meet, we shall not scape a brawl,
For now, these hot days, is the mad blood stirring.

MERCUTIO

Thou art like one of these fellows that, when
he enters the confines of a tavern, claps me his
sword upon the table and says "God send me
no need of thee!" and by the operation of the
second cup draws him on the drawer, when
indeed there is no need.

BENVOLIO
Am I like such a fellow?

MERCUTIO
Come, come, thou art as hot a jack in thy mood
as any in Italy; and as soon moved to be moody,
and as soon moody to be moved.

BENVOLIO
And what to?

MERCUTIO
Nay, an there were two such, we should have
none shortly, for one would kill the other. Thou!
why, thou wilt quarrel with a man that hath a
hair more or a hair less in his beard than thou
hast. Thou wilt quarrel with a man for cracking
nuts, having no other reason but because thou
hast hazel eyes. What eye but such an eye

would spy out such a quarrel? Thy head is as full of quarrels as an egg is full of meat; and yet thy head hath been beaten as addle as an egg for quarrelling. Thou hast quarrell'd with a man for coughing in the street, because he hath wakened thy dog that hath lain asleep in the sun. Didst thou not fall out with a tailor for wearing his new doublet before Easter, with another for tying his new shoes with an old riband? And yet thou wilt tutor me from quarrelling!

BENVOLIO

An I were so apt to quarrel as thou art, any man should buy the fee simple of my life for an hour and a quarter.

MERCUTIO

The fee simple? O simple!

Enter TYBALT *and others.*

BENVOLIO

By my head, here come the Capulets.

MERCUTIO

By my heel, I care not.

TYBALT

Follow me close, for I will speak to them.
Gentlemen, good den. A word with one of
    you.

MERCUTIO

And but one word with one of us? Couple it with
something; make it a word and a blow.

TYBALT

You shall find me apt enough to that, sir, an you will give me occasion.

MERCUTIO

Could you not take some occasion without giving?

TYBALT

Mercutio, thou consortest with Romeo.

MERCUTIO

Consort? What, dost thou make us minstrels? An thou make minstrels of us, look to hear nothing but discords. Here's my fiddlestick; here's that shall make you dance. Zounds, consort!

BENVOLIO

We talk here in the public haunt of men.

Either withdraw unto some private place

And reason coldly of your grievances,

Or else depart. Here all eyes gaze on us.

MERCUTIO

Men's eyes were made to look, and let them gaze.

I will not budge for no man's pleasure, I.

Enter ROMEO.

TYBALT

Well, peace be with you, sir. Here comes my man.

MERCUTIO

But I'll be hang'd, sir, if he wear your livery.

Marry, go before to field, he'll be your follower!

Your worship in that sense may call him man.

TYBALT

Romeo, the love I bear thee can afford
No better term than this: thou art a villain.

ROMEO

Tybalt, the reason that I have to love thee
Doth much excuse the appertaining rage
To such a greeting. Villain am I none.
Therefore farewell. I see thou knowest me not.

TYBALT

Boy, this shall not excuse the injuries
That thou hast done me; therefore turn and
  draw.

ROMEO

I do protest I never injur'd thee,
But love thee better than thou canst devise
Till thou shalt know the reason of my love;

And so good Capulet, which name I tender
As dearly as mine own, be satisfied.

MERCUTIO

O calm, dishonourable, vile submission!
Alla stoccata carries it away. *[Draws.]*
Tybalt, you ratcatcher, will you walk?

TYBALT

What wouldst thou have with me?

MERCUTIO

Good King of Cats, nothing but one of your nine
lives. That I mean to make bold withal, and, as
you shall use me hereafter, dry-beat the rest of
the eight. Will you pluck your sword out of his
pitcher by the ears? Make haste, lest mine be
about your ears ere it be out.

TYBALT

I am for you. *[Draws.]*

ROMEO

Gentle Mercutio, put thy rapier up.

MERCUTIO

Come, sir, your passado! *[They fight.]*

ROMEO

Draw, Benvolio; beat down their weapons.
Gentlemen, for shame! forbear this outrage!
Tybalt, Mercutio, the Prince expressly hath
Forbid this bandying in Verona streets.
Hold, Tybalt! Good Mercutio!

TYBALT *under* ROMEO's *arm thrusts* MERCUTIO *in, and flies with his* FOLLOWERS.

MERCUTIO

I am hurt.

A plague o' both your houses! I am sped.

Is he gone and hath nothing?

BENVOLIO

What, art thou hurt?

MERCUTIO

Ay, ay, a scratch, a scratch. Marry, 'tis enough.

Where is my page? Go, villain, fetch a surgeon.

Exit PAGE.

ROMEO

Courage, man. The hurt cannot be much.

MERCUTIO

No, 'tis not so deep as a well, nor so wide as a
church door; but 'tis enough, 'twill serve. Ask
for me to-morrow, and you shall find me a grave
man. I am peppered, I warrant, for this world.
A plague o' both your houses! Zounds, a dog, a
rat, a mouse, a cat, to scratch a man to death!
a braggart, a rogue, a villain, that fights by the
book of arithmetic! Why the devil came you
between us? I was hurt under your arm.

ROMEO

I thought all for the best.

MERCUTIO

Help me into some house, Benvolio,
Or I shall faint. A plague o' both your houses!
They have made worms' meat of me. I have it,
And soundly too. Your houses!

Exit, supported by BENVOLIO.

ROMEO

This gentleman, the Prince's near ally,
My very friend, hath got this mortal hurt
In my behalf—my reputation stain'd
With Tybalt's slander—Tybalt, that an hour
Hath been my kinsman. O sweet Juliet,
Thy beauty hath made me effeminate
And in my temper soft'ned valour's steel.

Enter BENVOLIO.

BENVOLIO

O Romeo, Romeo, brave Mercutio's dead!
That gallant spirit hath aspir'd the clouds,
Which too untimely here did scorn the earth.

ROMEO

This day's black fate on more days doth depend;
This but begins the woe others must end.

Enter TYBALT.

BENVOLIO

Here comes the furious Tybalt back again.

ROMEO

Alive in triumph, and Mercutio slain?
Away to heaven respective lenity,
And fire-ey'd fury be my conduct now!
Now, Tybalt, take the "villain" back again
That late thou gavest me; for Mercutio's soul
Is but a little way above our heads,
Staying for thine to keep him company.
Either thou or I, or both, must go with him.

TYBALT

Thou, wretched boy, that didst consort him here,
Shalt with him hence.

ROMEO

This shall determine that. *[They fight.* TYBALT *falls.]*

BENVOLIO

Romeo, away, be gone!

The citizens are up, and Tybalt slain.

Stand not amaz'd. The Prince will doom thee death

If thou art taken. Hence, be gone, away!

ROMEO

O, I am fortune's fool!

BENVOLIO

Why dost thou stay?

Exit ROMEO.

Enter CITIZENS.

CITIZEN

Which way ran he that kill'd Mercutio?

Tybalt, that murderer, which way ran he?

BENVOLIO

There lies that Tybalt.

CITIZEN

Up, sir, go with me.

I charge thee in the Prince's name obey.

Enter PRINCE *[attended]*, OLD MONTAGUE, CAPULET,

LADY MONTAGUE, LADY CAPULET, *and others.*

PRINCE

Where are the vile beginners of this fray?

BENVOLIO

O noble Prince. I can discover all

The unlucky manage of this fatal brawl.
There lies the man, slain by young Romeo,
That slew thy kinsman, brave Mercutio.

LADY CAPULET

Tybalt, my cousin! O my brother's child!
O Prince! O husband! O, the blood is spill'd
Of my dear kinsman! Prince, as thou art true,
For blood of ours shed blood of Montague.
O cousin, cousin!

PRINCE

Benvolio, who began this bloody fray?

BENVOLIO

Tybalt, here slain, whom Romeo's hand did stay.
Romeo, that spoke him fair, bid him bethink
How nice the quarrel was, and urg'd withal
Your high displeasure. All this—uttered

With gentle breath, calm look, knees humbly
    bow'd—
Could not take truce with the unruly spleen
Of Tybalt deaf to peace, but that he tilts
With piercing steel at bold Mercutio's breast;
Who, all as hot, turns deadly point to point,
And, with a martial scorn, with one hand beats
Cold death aside and with the other sends
It back to Tybalt, whose dexterity
Retorts it. Romeo he cries aloud,
"Hold, friends! friends, part!" and swifter than
    his tongue,
His agile arm beats down their fatal points,
And 'twixt them rushes; underneath whose arm
An envious thrust from Tybalt hit the life
Of stout Mercutio, and then Tybalt fled;
But by-and-by comes back to Romeo,
Who had but newly entertain'd revenge,
And to't they go like lightning; for, ere I
Could draw to part them, was stout Tybalt slain;
And, as he fell, did Romeo turn and fly.
This is the truth, or let Benvolio die.

Lady Capulet

He is a kinsman to the Montague;
Affection makes him false, he speaks not true.
Some twenty of them fought in this black strife,
And all those twenty could but kill one life.
I beg for justice, which thou, Prince, must give.
Romeo slew Tybalt; Romeo must not live.

Prince

Romeo slew him; he slew Mercutio.
Who now the price of his dear blood doth owe?

Montague

Not Romeo, Prince; he was Mercutio's friend;
His fault concludes but what the law should end,
The life of Tybalt.

Prince

And for that offence
Immediately we do exile him hence.

I have an interest in your hate's proceeding,

My blood for your rude brawls doth lie

    a-bleeding;

But I'll amerce you with so strong a fine

That you shall all repent the loss of mine.

I will be deaf to pleading and excuses;

Nor tears nor prayers shall purchase out abuses.

Therefore use none. Let Romeo hence in haste,

Else, when he is found, that hour is his last.

Bear hence this body, and attend our will.

Mercy but murders, pardoning those that kill.

Exeunt.

SCENE II.

Enter JULIET *alone*.

JULIET
Gallop apace, you fiery-footed steeds,
Towards Phoebus' lodging! Such a wagoner
As Phaeton would whip you to the West
And bring in cloudy night immediately.
Spread thy close curtain, love-performing night,
That runaway eyes may wink, and Romeo
Leap to these arms untalk'd of and unseen.
Lovers can see to do their amorous rites
By their own beauties; or, if love be blind,
It best agrees with night. Come, civil night,
Thou sober-suited matron, all in black,
And learn me how to lose a winning match,
Play'd for a pair of stainless maidenhoods.
Hood my unmann'd blood, bating in my cheeks,

With thy black mantle till strange love, grown
    bold,
Think true love acted simple modesty.
Come, night; come, Romeo; come, thou day in
    night;
For thou wilt lie upon the wings of night
Whiter than new snow upon a raven's back.
Come, gentle night; come, loving, black-brow'd
    night;
Give me my Romeo; and, when he shall die,
Take him and cut him out in little stars,
And he will make the face of heaven so fine
That all the world will be in love with night
And pay no worship to the garish sun.
O, I have bought the mansion of a love,
But not possess'd it; and though I am sold,
Not yet enjoy'd. So tedious is this day
As is the night before some festival
To an impatient child that hath new robes
And may not wear them. O, here comes my
    nurse,

Enter Nurse, *with cords.*

And she brings news; and every tongue that
    speaks
But Romeo's name speaks heavenly eloquence.
Now, Nurse, what news? What hast thou there?
    the cords
That Romeo bid thee fetch?

Nurse

Ay, ay, the cords. *[Throws them down.]*

Juliet

Ay me! what news? Why dost thou wring thy
    hands?

Nurse

Ah, weraday! he's dead, he's dead, he's dead!
We are undone, lady, we are undone!

Alack the day! he's gone, he's kill'd, he's
   dead!

JULIET
Can heaven be so envious?

NURSE
Romeo can,
Though heaven cannot. O Romeo, Romeo!
Who ever would have thought it? Romeo!

JULIET
What devil art thou that dost torment me thus?
This torture should be roar'd in dismal hell.
Hath Romeo slain himself? Say thou but "I,"
And that bare vowel "I" shall poison more
Than the death-darting eye of cockatrice.
I am not I, if there be such an "I";
Or those eyes shut that make thee answer "I."

If be be slain, say "I"; or if not, "no."
Brief sounds determine of my weal or woe.

NURSE

I saw the wound, I saw it with mine eyes,
(God save the mark!) here on his manly breast.
A piteous corse, a bloody piteous corse;
Pale, pale as ashes, all bedaub'd in blood,
All in gore-blood. I swounded at the sight.

JULIET

O, break, my heart! poor bankrout, break at once!
To prison, eyes; ne'er look on liberty!
Vile earth, to earth resign; end motion here,
And thou and Romeo press one heavy bier!

NURSE

O Tybalt, Tybalt, the best friend I had!
O courteous Tybalt! honest gentleman
That ever I should live to see thee dead!

JULIET

What storm is this that blows so contrary?
Is Romeo slaught'red, and is Tybalt dead?
My dear-lov'd cousin, and my dearer lord?
Then, dreadful trumpet, sound the general
 doom!
For who is living, if those two are gone?

NURSE

Tybalt is gone, and Romeo banished;
Romeo that kill'd him, he is banished.

JULIET

O God! Did Romeo's hand shed Tybalt's blood?

NURSE

It did, it did! alas the day, it did!

William Shakespeare

JULIET

O serpent heart, hid with a flow'ring face!

Did ever dragon keep so fair a cave?

Beautiful tyrant! fiend angelical!

Dove-feather'd raven! wolvish-ravening lamb!

Despised substance of divinest show!

Just opposite to what thou justly seem'st—

A damned saint, an honourable villain!

O nature, what hadst thou to do in hell

When thou didst bower the spirit of a fiend

In mortal paradise of such sweet flesh?

Was ever book containing such vile matter

So fairly bound? O, that deceit should dwell

In such a gorgeous palace!

NURSE

There's no trust,

No faith, no honesty in men; all perjur'd,

All forsworn, all naught, all dissemblers.

Ah, where's my man? Give me some aqua vitae.

These griefs, these woes, these sorrows make
   me old.
Shame come to Romeo!

JULIET

Blister'd be thy tongue
For such a wish! He was not born to shame.
Upon his brow shame is asham'd to sit;
For 'tis a throne where honour may be crown'd
Sole monarch of the universal earth.
O, what a beast was I to chide at him!

NURSE

Will you speak well of him that kill'd your cousin?

JULIET

Shall I speak ill of him that is my husband?
Ah, poor my lord, what tongue shall smooth thy
   name

When I, thy three-hours wife, have mangled it?
But wherefore, villain, didst thou kill my cousin?
That villain cousin would have kill'd my
    husband.
Back, foolish tears, back to your native spring!
Your tributary drops belong to woe,
Which you, mistaking, offer up to joy.
My husband lives, that Tybalt would have slain;
And Tybalt's dead, that would have slain my
    husband.
All this is comfort; wherefore weep I then?
Some word there was, worser than Tybalt's
    death,
That murd'red me. I would forget it fain;
But O, it presses to my memory
Like damned guilty deeds to sinners' minds!
"Tybalt is dead, and Romeo—banished."
That "banished," that one word "banished,"
Hath slain ten thousand Tybalts. Tybalt's death
Was woe enough, if it had ended there;
Or, if sour woe delights in fellowship
And needly will be rank'd with other griefs,

Why followed not, when she said "Tybalt's dead,"
Thy father, or thy mother, nay, or both,
Which modern lamentation might have mov'd?
But with a rearward following Tybalt's death,
"Romeo is banished"— to speak that word
Is father, mother, Tybalt, Romeo, Juliet,
All slain, all dead. "Romeo is banished"—
There is no end, no limit, measure, bound,
In that word's death; no words can that woe
    sound.
Where is my father and my mother, Nurse?

NURSE

Weeping and wailing over Tybalt's corse.
Will you go to them? I will bring you thither.

JULIET

Wash they his wounds with tears? Mine shall be
    spent,
When theirs are dry, for Romeo's banishment.

Take up those cords. Poor ropes, you are beguil'd,
Both you and I, for Romeo is exil'd.
He made you for a highway to my bed;
But I, a maid, die maiden-widowed.
Come, cords; come, Nurse; I'll to my wedding
    bed;
And death, not Romeo, take my maidenhead!

NURSE

Hie to your chamber. I'll find Romeo
To comfort you. I wot well where he is.
Hark ye, your Romeo will be here at night.
I'll to him; he is hid at Laurence's cell.

JULIET

O, find him! give this ring to my true knight
And bid him come to take his last farewell.

Exeunt.

SCENE III.

FRIAR LAURENCE'S *cell*.

Enter FRIAR LAURENCE.

FRIAR LAURENCE

Romeo, come forth; come forth, thou fearful man.
Affliction is enamour'd of thy parts,
And thou art wedded to calamity.

Enter ROMEO.

ROMEO

Father, what news? What is the Prince's doom?
What sorrow craves acquaintance at my hand
That I yet know not?

FRIAR LAURENCE

Too familiar

Is my dear son with such sour company.
I bring thee tidings of the Prince's doom.

ROMEO
What less than doomsday is the Prince's doom?

FRIAR LAURENCE
A gentler judgment vanish'd from his lips—
Not body's death, but body's banishment.

ROMEO
Ha, banishment? Be merciful, say "death";
For exile hath more terror in his look,
Much more than death. Do not say "banishment."

FRIAR LAURENCE
Hence from Verona art thou banished.
Be patient, for the world is broad and wide.

ROMEO

There is no world without Verona walls,
But purgatory, torture, hell itself.
Hence banished is banish'd from the world,
And world's exile is death. Then "banishment"
Is death misterm'd. Calling death "banishment,"
Thou cut'st my head off with a golden axe
And smilest upon the stroke that murders me.

FRIAR LAURENCE

O deadly sin! O rude unthankfulness!
Thy fault our law calls death; but the kind Prince,
Taking thy part, hath rush'd aside the law,
And turn'd that black word death to banishment.
This is dear mercy, and thou seest it not.

ROMEO

'Tis torture, and not mercy. Heaven is here,
Where Juliet lives; and every cat and dog
And little mouse, every unworthy thing,

Live here in heaven and may look on her;
But Romeo may not. More validity,
More honourable state, more courtship lives
In carrion flies than Romeo. They may seize
On the white wonder of dear Juliet's hand
And steal immortal blessing from her lips,
Who, even in pure and vestal modesty,
Still blush, as thinking their own kisses sin;
But Romeo may not—he is banished.
This may flies do, when I from this must fly;
They are free men, but I am banished.
And sayest thou yet that exile is not death?
Hadst thou no poison mix'd, no sharp-ground
   knife,
No sudden mean of death, though ne'er so mean,
But "banished" to kill me—"banished"?
O friar, the damned use that word in hell;
Howling attends it! How hast thou the heart,
Being a divine, a ghostly confessor,
A sin-absolver, and my friend profess'd,
To mangle me with that word "banished"?

FRIAR LAURENCE

Thou fond mad man, hear me a little speak.

ROMEO

O, thou wilt speak again of banishment.

FRIAR LAURENCE

I'll give thee armour to keep off that word;
Adversity's sweet milk, philosophy,
To comfort thee, though thou art banished.

ROMEO

Yet "banished"? Hang up philosophy!
Unless philosophy can make a Juliet,
Displant a town, reverse a prince's doom,
It helps not, it prevails not. Talk no more.

FRIAR LAURENCE

O, then I see that madmen have no ears.

ROMEO

How should they, when that wise men have no
    eyes?

FRIAR LAURENCE

Let me dispute with thee of thy estate.

ROMEO

Thou canst not speak of that thou dost not
    feel.

Wert thou as young as I, Juliet thy love,

An hour but married, Tybalt murdered,

Doting like me, and like me banished,

Then mightst thou speak, then mightst thou tear
    thy hair,

And fall upon the ground, as I do now,

Taking the measure of an unmade grave.

[Knock within.]

FRIAR LAURENCE

Arise; one knocks. Good Romeo, hide thyself.

ROMEO

Not I; unless the breath of heartsick groans,
Mist-like infold me from the search of eyes.
[Knock.]

FRIAR LAURENCE

Hark, how they knock! Who's there? Romeo,
    arise;
Thou wilt be taken.—Stay awhile!—Stand up;
    [Knock.]
Run to my study.—By-and-by!—God's will,
What simpleness is this.—I come, I come!
    [Knock.]
Who knocks so hard? Whence come you? What's
    your will?

NURSE

[within] Let me come in, and you shall know my
  errand.
I come from Lady Juliet.

FRIAR LAURENCE
Welcome then.

Enter Nurse.

NURSE
O holy friar, O, tell me, holy friar
Where is my lady's lord, where's Romeo?

FRIAR LAURENCE
There on the ground, with his own tears made
  drunk.

NURSE

O, he is even in my mistress' case,
Just in her case!

FRIAR LAURENCE

O woeful sympathy!
Piteous predicament!

NURSE

Even so lies she,
Blubb'ring and weeping, weeping and
    blubbering.
Stand up, stand up! Stand, an you be a man.
For Juliet's sake, for her sake, rise and stand!
Why should you fall into so deep an O?

ROMEO

[rises] Nurse—

NURSE

Ah sir! ah sir! Well, death's the end of all.

ROMEO

Spakest thou of Juliet? How is it with her?
Doth not she think me an old murderer,
Now I have stain'd the childhood of our joy
With blood remov'd but little from her own?
Where is she? and how doth she! and what says
My conceal'd lady to our cancell'd love?

NURSE

O, she says nothing, sir, but weeps and weeps;
And now falls on her bed, and then starts up,
And Tybalt calls; and then on Romeo cries,
And then down falls again.

ROMEO

As if that name,

Shot from the deadly level of a gun,

Did murder her; as that name's cursed hand

Murder'd her kinsman. O, tell me, friar, tell me,

In what vile part of this anatomy

Doth my name lodge? Tell me, that I may sack

The hateful mansion. *[Draws his dagger.]*

FRIAR LAURENCE

Hold thy desperate hand.

Art thou a man? Thy form cries out thou art;

Thy tears are womanish, thy wild acts denote

The unreasonable fury of a beast.

Unseemly woman in a seeming man!

Or ill-beseeming beast in seeming both!

Thou hast amaz'd me. By my holy order,

I thought thy disposition better temper'd.

Hast thou slain Tybalt? Wilt thou slay thyself?

And slay thy lady that in thy life lives,

By doing damned hate upon thyself?

Why railest thou on thy birth, the heaven, and

earth?

Since birth and heaven and earth, all three do
    meet
In thee at once; which thou at once wouldst
    lose.
Fie, fie, thou shamest thy shape, thy love, thy wit,
Which, like a usurer, abound'st in all,
And usest none in that true use indeed
Which should bedeck thy shape, thy love, thy
    wit.
Thy noble shape is but a form of wax
Digressing from the valour of a man;
Thy dear love sworn but hollow perjury,
Killing that love which thou hast vow'd to
    cherish;
Thy wit, that ornament to shape and love,
Misshapen in the conduct of them both,
Like powder in a skilless soldier's flask,
Is set afire by thine own ignorance,
And thou dismemb'red with thine own defence.
What, rouse thee, man! Thy Juliet is alive,
For whose dear sake thou wast but lately dead.
There art thou happy. Tybalt would kill thee,

But thou slewest Tybalt. There art thou happy too.

The law, that threat'ned death, becomes thy
friend

And turns it to exile. There art thou happy.

A pack of blessings light upon thy back;

Happiness courts thee in her best array;

But, like a misbehav'd and sullen wench,

Thou pout'st upon thy fortune and thy love.

Take heed, take heed, for such die miserable.

Go get thee to thy love, as was decreed,

Ascend her chamber, hence and comfort her.

But look thou stay not till the watch be set,

For then thou canst not pass to Mantua,

Where thou shalt live till we can find a time

To blaze your marriage, reconcile your friends,

Beg pardon of the Prince, and call thee back

With twenty hundred thousand times more joy

Than thou went'st forth in lamentation.

Go before, Nurse. Commend me to thy lady,

And bid her hasten all the house to bed,

Which heavy sorrow makes them apt unto.

Romeo is coming.

NURSE

O Lord, I could have stay'd here all the night
To hear good counsel. O, what learning is!
My lord, I'll tell my lady you will come.

ROMEO

Do so, and bid my sweet prepare to chide.

NURSE

Here is a ring she bid me give you, sir.
Hie you, make haste, for it grows very late.

Exit.

ROMEO

How well my comfort is reviv'd by this!

FRIAR LAURENCE

Go hence; good night; and here stands all your
     state:
Either be gone before the watch be set,
Or by the break of day disguis'd from hence.
Sojourn in Mantua. I'll find out your man,
And he shall signify from time to time
Every good hap to you that chances here.
Give me thy hand. 'Tis late. Farewell; good night.

ROMEO

But that a joy past joy calls out on me,
It were a grief so brief to part with thee.
Farewell.

Exeunt.

SCENE IV.

CAPULET's *house*

Enter OLD CAPULET, LADY CAPULET, *and* PARIS.

CAPULET

Things have fall'n out, sir, so unluckily
That we have had no time to move our
    daughter.
Look you, she lov'd her kinsman Tybalt dearly,
And so did I. Well, we were born to die.
'Tis very late; she'll not come down to-night.
I promise you, but for your company,
I would have been abed an hour ago.

PARIS

These times of woe afford no tune to woo.
Madam, good night. Commend me to your
    daughter.

LADY CAPULET

I will, and know her mind early to-morrow;
To-night she's mew'd up to her heaviness.

CAPULET

Sir Paris, I will make a desperate tender
Of my child's love. I think she will be rul'd
In all respects by me; nay more, I doubt it not.
Wife, go you to her ere you go to bed;
Acquaint her here of my son Paris' love
And bid her (mark you me?) on Wednesday next—
But, soft! what day is this?

PARIS

Monday, my lord.

CAPULET

Monday! ha, ha! Well, Wednesday is too soon.
Thursday let it be—a Thursday, tell her
She shall be married to this noble earl.

Will you be ready? Do you like this haste?
We'll keep no great ado—a friend or two;
For hark you, Tybalt being slain so late,
It may be thought we held him carelessly,
Being our kinsman, if we revel much.
Therefore we'll have some half a dozen friends,
And there an end. But what say you to Thursday?

PARIS
My lord, I would that Thursday were to-morrow.

CAPULET
Well, get you gone. A Thursday be it then.
Go you to Juliet ere you go to bed;
Prepare her, wife, against this wedding day.
Farewell, My lord.—Light to my chamber, ho!
Afore me, It is so very very late
That we may call it early by-and-by.
Good night.

Exeunt.

SCENE V.

CAPULET's *orchard.*

Enter Romeo and Juliet aloft, at the window.

JULIET

Wilt thou be gone? It is not yet near day.
It was the nightingale, and not the lark,
That pierc'd the fearful hollow of thine ear.
Nightly she sings on yond pomegranate tree.
Believe me, love, it was the nightingale.

ROMEO

It was the lark, the herald of the morn;
No nightingale. Look, love, what envious streaks
Do lace the severing clouds in yonder East.
Night's candles are burnt out, and jocund day
Stands tiptoe on the misty mountain tops.
I must be gone and live, or stay and die.

JULIET

Yond light is not daylight; I know it, I.

It is some meteor that the sun exhales

To be to thee this night a torchbearer

And light thee on the way to Mantua.

Therefore stay yet; thou need'st not to be gone.

ROMEO

Let me be ta'en, let me be put to death.

I am content, so thou wilt have it so.

I'll say yon grey is not the morning's eye,

'Tis but the pale reflex of Cynthia's brow;

Nor that is not the lark whose notes do beat

The vaulty heaven so high above our heads.

I have more care to stay than will to go.

Come, death, and welcome! Juliet wills it so.

How is't, my soul? Let's talk; it is not day.

JULIET

It is, it is! Hie hence, be gone, away!

It is the lark that sings so out of tune,

Straining harsh discords and unpleasing sharps.

Some say the lark makes sweet division;

This doth not so, for she divideth us.

Some say the lark and loathed toad chang'd
    eyes;

O, now I would they had chang'd voices too,

Since arm from arm that voice doth us affray,

Hunting thee hence with hunt's-up to the day!

O, now be gone! More light and light it grows.

ROMEO

More light and light—more dark and dark our
    woes!

Enter NURSE.

NURSE

Madam!

JULIET

Nurse?

NURSE

Your lady mother is coming to your chamber.
The day is broke; be wary, look about.

JULIET

Then, window, let day in, and let life out.

Exit.

ROMEO

Farewell, farewell! One kiss, and I'll descend.

[He goeth down.]

JULIET

Art thou gone so, my lord, my love, my friend?
I must hear from thee every day in the hour,

For in a minute there are many days.
O, by this count I shall be much in years
Ere I again behold my Romeo!

ROMEO

Farewell!
I will omit no opportunity
That may convey my greetings, love, to thee.

JULIET

O, think'st thou we shall ever meet again?

ROMEO

I doubt it not; and all these woes shall serve
For sweet discourses in our time to come.

JULIET

O God, I have an ill-divining soul!

Methinks I see thee, now thou art below,
As one dead in the bottom of a tomb.
Either my eyesight fails, or thou look'st pale.

ROMEO
And trust me, love, in my eye so do you.
Dry sorrow drinks our blood. Adieu, adieu!

Exit.

JULIET
O Fortune, Fortune! all men call thee fickle.
If thou art fickle, what dost thou with him
That is renown'd for faith? Be fickle, Fortune,
For then I hope thou wilt not keep him long
But send him back.

LADY CAPULET
[within] Ho, daughter! are you up?

JULIET

Who is't that calls? It is my lady mother.

Is she not down so late, or up so early?

What unaccustom'd cause procures her hither?

Enter LADY CAPULET.

LADY CAPULET

Why, how now, Juliet?

JULIET

Madam, I am not well.

LADY CAPULET

Evermore weeping for your cousin's death?

What, wilt thou wash him from his grave with
    tears?

An if thou couldst, thou couldst not make him
    live.

Therefore have done. Some grief shows much of
    love;
But much of grief shows still some want of wit.

    JULIET
Yet let me weep for such a feeling loss.

    LADY CAPULET
So shall you feel the loss, but not the friend
Which you weep for.

    JULIET
Feeling so the loss,
I cannot choose but ever weep the friend.

    LADY CAPULET
Well, girl, thou weep'st not so much for his death
As that the villain lives which slaughter'd him.

JULIET
What villain, madam?

LADY CAPULET
That same villain Romeo.

JULIET
[aside] Villain and he be many miles asunder.—
God pardon him! I do, with all my heart;
And yet no man like he doth grieve my heart.

LADY CAPULET
That is because the traitor murderer lives.

JULIET
Ay, madam, from the reach of these my hands.
Would none but I might venge my cousin's
     death!

William Shakespeare

LADY CAPULET

We will have vengeance for it, fear thou not.
Then weep no more. I'll send to one in Mantua,
Where that same banish'd runagate doth live,
Shall give him such an unaccustom'd dram
That he shall soon keep Tybalt company;
And then I hope thou wilt be satisfied.

JULIET

Indeed I never shall be satisfied
With Romeo till I behold him—dead—
Is my poor heart so for a kinsman vex'd.
Madam, if you could find out but a man
To bear a poison, I would temper it;
That Romeo should, upon receipt thereof,
Soon sleep in quiet. O, how my heart abhors
To hear him nam'd and cannot come to him,
To wreak the love I bore my cousin Tybalt
Upon his body that hath slaughter'd him!

LADY CAPULET

Find thou the means, and I'll find such a man.

But now I'll tell thee joyful tidings, girl.

JULIET

And joy comes well in such a needy time.

What are they, I beseech your ladyship?

LADY CAPULET

Well, well, thou hast a careful father, child;

One who, to put thee from thy heaviness,

Hath sorted out a sudden day of joy

That thou expects not nor I look'd not for.

JULIET

Madam, in happy time! What day is that?

LADY CAPULET

Marry, my child, early next Thursday morn
The gallant, young, and noble gentleman,
The County Paris, at Saint Peter's Church,
Shall happily make thee there a joyful bride.

JULIET

Now by Saint Peter's Church, and Peter too,
He shall not make me there a joyful bride!
I wonder at this haste, that I must wed
Ere he that should be husband comes to woo.
I pray you tell my lord and father, madam,
I will not marry yet; and when I do, I swear
It shall be Romeo, whom you know I hate,
Rather than Paris. These are news indeed!

LADY CAPULET

Here comes your father. Tell him so yourself,
And see how he will take it at your hands.

Enter Capulet *and* Nurse.

CAPULET

When the sun sets the air doth drizzle dew,
But for the sunset of my brother's son
It rains downright.
How now? a conduit, girl? What, still in tears?
Evermore show'ring? In one little body
Thou counterfeit'st a bark, a sea, a wind:
For still thy eyes, which I may call the sea,
Do ebb and flow with tears; the bark thy body is
Sailing in this salt flood; the winds, thy sighs,
Who, raging with thy tears and they with them,
Without a sudden calm will overset
Thy tempest-tossed body. How now, wife?
Have you delivered to her our decree?

LADY CAPULET

Ay, sir; but she will none, she gives you thanks.
I would the fool were married to her grave!

CAPULET

Soft! take me with you, take me with you, wife.
How? Will she none? Doth she not give us
    thanks?
Is she not proud? Doth she not count her blest,
Unworthy as she is, that we have wrought
So worthy a gentleman to be her bridegroom?

JULIET

Not proud you have, but thankful that you have.
Proud can I never be of what I hate,
But thankful even for hate that is meant love.

CAPULET

How, how, how, how, choplogic? What is this?
"Proud"—and "I thank you"—and "I thank you
    not"—
And yet "not proud"? Mistress minion you,
Thank me no thankings, nor proud me no
    prouds,

But fettle your fine joints 'gainst Thursday next

To go with Paris to Saint Peter's Church,

Or I will drag thee on a hurdle thither.

Out, you green-sickness carrion I out, you

    baggage!

You tallow-face!

Lady Capulet

Fie, fie! what, are you mad?

Juliet

Good father, I beseech you on my knees,

Hear me with patience but to speak a word.

Capulet

Hang thee, young baggage! disobedient wretch!

I tell thee what—get thee to church a Thursday

Or never after look me in the face.

Speak not, reply not, do not answer me!

My fingers itch. Wife, we scarce thought us
    blest
That God had lent us but this only child;
But now I see this one is one too much,
And that we have a curse in having her.
Out on her, hilding!

NURSE

God in heaven bless her!
You are to blame, my lord, to rate her so.

CAPULET

And why, my Lady Wisdom? Hold your tongue,
Good Prudence. Smatter with your gossips, go!

NURSE

I speak no treason.

CAPULET

O, God-i-god-en!

NURSE

May not one speak?

CAPULET

Peace, you mumbling fool!

Utter your gravity o'er a gossip's bowl,

For here we need it not.

LADY CAPULET

You are too hot.

CAPULET

God's bread! It makes me mad. Day, night, late,
    early,

At home, abroad, alone, in company,

Waking or sleeping, still my care hath been
To have her match'd; and having now provided
A gentleman of princely parentage,
Of fair demesnes, youthful, and nobly train'd,
Stuff'd, as they say, with honourable parts,
Proportion'd as one's thought would wish a man—
And then to have a wretched puling fool,
A whining mammet, in her fortune's tender,
To answer "I'll not wed, I cannot love;
I am too young, I pray you pardon me"!
But, an you will not wed, I'll pardon you.
Graze where you will, you shall not house with me.
Look to't, think on't; I do not use to jest.
Thursday is near; lay hand on heart, advise:
An you be mine, I'll give you to my friend;
An you be not, hang, beg, starve, die in the
     streets,
For, by my soul, I'll ne'er acknowledge thee,
Nor what is mine shall never do thee good.
Trust to't. Bethink you. I'll not be forsworn.

Exit.

JULIET

Is there no pity sitting in the clouds

That sees into the bottom of my grief?

O sweet my mother, cast me not away!

Delay this marriage for a month, a week;

Or if you do not, make the bridal bed

In that dim monument where Tybalt lies.

LADY CAPULET

Talk not to me, for I'll not speak a word.

Do as thou wilt, for I have done with thee.

Exit.

JULIET

O God!—O Nurse, how shall this be prevented?

My husband is on earth, my faith in heaven.

How shall that faith return again to earth

Unless that husband send it me from heaven

By leaving earth? Comfort me, counsel me.

Alack, alack, that heaven should practise
    stratagems
Upon so soft a subject as myself!
What say'st thou? Hast thou not a word of joy?
Some comfort, Nurse.

NURSE
Faith, here it is.
Romeo is banish'd; and all the world to nothing
That he dares ne'er come back to challenge you;
Or if he do, it needs must be by stealth.
Then, since the case so stands as now it doth,
I think it best you married with the County.
O, he's a lovely gentleman!
Romeo's a dishclout to him. An eagle, madam,
Hath not so green, so quick, so fair an eye
As Paris hath. Beshrew my very heart,
I think you are happy in this second match,
For it excels your first; or if it did not,
Your first is dead—or 'twere as good he were
As living here and you no use of him.

JULIET

Speak'st thou this from thy heart?

NURSE

And from my soul too; else beshrew them both.

JULIET

Amen!

NURSE

What?

JULIET

Well, thou hast comforted me marvellous much.
Go in; and tell my lady I am gone,
Having displeas'd my father, to Laurence's cell,
To make confession and to be absolv'd.

NURSE

Marry, I will; and this is wisely done.

Exit.

JULIET

Ancient damnation! O most wicked fiend!
Is it more sin to wish me thus forsworn,
Or to dispraise my lord with that same tongue
Which she hath prais'd him with above compare
So many thousand times? Go, counsellor!
Thou and my bosom henceforth shall be twain.
I'll to the friar to know his remedy.
If all else fail, myself have power to die.

Exit.

ACT IV.

SCENE I.

Enter FRIAR LAURENCE *and* COUNTY PARIS.

FRIAR LAURENCE
On Thursday, sir? The time is very short.

PARIS
My father Capulet will have it so,
And I am nothing slow to slack his haste.

FRIAR LAURENCE
You say you do not know the lady's mind.
Uneven is the course; I like it not.

PARIS

Immoderately she weeps for Tybalt's death,

And therefore have I little talk'd of love;

For Venus smiles not in a house of tears.

Now, sir, her father counts it dangerous

That she do give her sorrow so much sway,

And in his wisdom hastes our marriage

To stop the inundation of her tears,

Which, too much minded by herself alone,

May be put from her by society.

Now do you know the reason of this haste.

FRIAR LAURENCE

[aside] I would I knew not why it should be
 slow'd.—

Look, sir, here comes the lady toward my cell.

Enter JULIET.

PARIS

Happily met, my lady and my wife!

JULIET

That may be, sir, when I may be a wife.

PARIS

That may be must be, love, on Thursday next.

JULIET

What must be shall be.

FRIAR LAURENCE

That's a certain text.

PARIS

Come you to make confession to this father?

JULIET

To answer that, I should confess to you.

PARIS

Do not deny to him that you love me.

JULIET

I will confess to you that I love him.

PARIS

So will ye, I am sure, that you love me.

JULIET

If I do so, it will be of more price,
Being spoke behind your back, than to your
    face.

PARIS

Poor soul, thy face is much abus'd with tears.

JULIET

The tears have got small victory by that,
For it was bad enough before their spite.

PARIS

Thou wrong'st it more than tears with that
    report.

JULIET

That is no slander, sir, which is a truth;
And what I spake, I spake it to my face.

PARIS

Thy face is mine, and thou hast sland'red it.

JULIET

It may be so, for it is not mine own.
Are you at leisure, holy father, now,
Or shall I come to you at evening mass?

FRIAR LAURENCE

My leisure serves me, pensive daughter, now.
My lord, we must entreat the time alone.

PARIS

God shield I should disturb devotion!
Juliet, on Thursday early will I rouse ye.
Till then, adieu, and keep this holy kiss.

Exit.

JULIET

O, shut the door! and when thou hast done so,
Come weep with me—past hope, past cure, past
  help!

FRIAR LAURENCE

Ah, Juliet, I already know thy grief;

It strains me past the compass of my wits.

I hear thou must, and nothing may prorogue it,

On Thursday next be married to this County.

JULIET

Tell me not, friar, that thou hear'st of this,

Unless thou tell me how I may prevent it.

If in thy wisdom thou canst give no help,

Do thou but call my resolution wise

And with this knife I'll help it presently.

God join'd my heart and Romeo's, thou our
hands;

And ere this hand, by thee to Romeo's seal'd,

Shall be the label to another deed,

Or my true heart with treacherous revolt

Turn to another, this shall slay them both.

Therefore, out of thy long-experienc'd time,

Give me some present counsel; or, behold,

'Twixt my extremes and me this bloody knife

Shall play the empire, arbitrating that

Which the commission of thy years and art

Could to no issue of true honour bring.

Be not so long to speak. I long to die

If what thou speak'st speak not of remedy.

FRIAR LAURENCE

Hold, daughter. I do spy a kind of hope,

Which craves as desperate an execution

As that is desperate which we would prevent.

If, rather than to marry County Paris

Thou hast the strength of will to slay thyself,

Then is it likely thou wilt undertake

A thing like death to chide away this shame,

That cop'st with death himself to scape from it;

And, if thou dar'st, I'll give thee remedy.

JULIET

O, bid me leap, rather than marry Paris,

From off the battlements of yonder tower,

Or walk in thievish ways, or bid me lurk

Where serpents are; chain me with roaring
    bears,

Or shut me nightly in a charnel house,

O'ercover'd quite with dead men's rattling bones,

With reeky shanks and yellow chapless skulls;

Or bid me go into a new-made grave

And hide me with a dead man in his shroud—

Things that, to hear them told, have made me
    tremble—

And I will do it without fear or doubt,

To live an unstain'd wife to my sweet love.

FRIAR LAURENCE

Hold, then. Go home, be merry, give consent

To marry Paris. Wednesday is to-morrow.

To-morrow night look that thou lie alone;

Let not the nurse lie with thee in thy chamber.

Take thou this vial, being then in bed,

And this distilled liquor drink thou off;

When presently through all thy veins shall run

A cold and drowsy humour; for no pulse
Shall keep his native progress, but surcease;
No warmth, no breath, shall testify thou livest;
The roses in thy lips and cheeks shall fade
To paly ashes, thy eyes' windows fall
Like death when he shuts up the day of life;
Each part, depriv'd of supple government,
Shall, stiff and stark and cold, appear like death;
And in this borrowed likeness of shrunk death
Thou shalt continue two-and-forty hours,
And then awake as from a pleasant sleep.
Now, when the bridegroom in the morning
    comes
To rouse thee from thy bed, there art thou dead.
Then, as the manner of our country is,
In thy best robes uncovered on the bier
Thou shalt be borne to that same ancient vault
Where all the kindred of the Capulets lie.
In the meantime, against thou shalt awake,
Shall Romeo by my letters know our drift;
And hither shall he come; and he and I
Will watch thy waking, and that very night

Shall Romeo bear thee hence to Mantua.

And this shall free thee from this present shame,

If no inconstant toy nor womanish fear

Abate thy valour in the acting it.

JULIET

Give me, give me! O, tell not me of fear!

FRIAR LAURENCE

Hold! Get you gone, be strong and prosperous

In this resolve. I'll send a friar with speed

To Mantua, with my letters to thy lord.

JULIET

Love give me strength! and strength shall help

　　afford.

Farewell, dear father.

Exeunt.

SCENE II.

CAPULET's *house.*

Enter CAPULET, LADY CAPULET, NURSE, *and*
SERVINGMEN, *two or three.*

CAPULET

So many guests invite as here are writ.

Exit a Servingman.

Sirrah, go hire me twenty cunning cooks.

SERVINGMAN

You shall have none ill, sir; for I'll try if they can
lick their fingers.

CAPULET

How canst thou try them so?

SERVINGMAN
Marry, sir, 'tis an ill cook that cannot lick his
own fingers. Therefore he that cannot lick his
fingers goes not with me.

CAPULET
Go, begone.

Exit Servingman.

We shall be much unfurnish'd for this time.
What, is my daughter gone to Friar Laurence?

NURSE
Ay, forsooth.

CAPULET
Well, be may chance to do some good on her.
A peevish self-will'd harlotry it is.

Enter JULIET.

NURSE

See where she comes from shrift with merry
look.

CAPULET

How now, my headstrong? Where have you been
gadding?

JULIET

Where I have learnt me to repent the sin
Of disobedient opposition
To you and your behests, and am enjoin'd
By holy Laurence to fall prostrate here
To beg your pardon. Pardon, I beseech you!
Henceforward I am ever rul'd by you.

CAPULET

Send for the County. Go tell him of this.

I'll have this knot knit up to-morrow morning.

JULIET

I met the youthful lord at Laurence's cell

And gave him what becomed love I might,

Not stepping o'er the bounds of modesty.

CAPULET

Why, I am glad on't. This is well. Stand up.

This is as't should be. Let me see the County.

Ay, marry, go, I say, and fetch him hither.

Now, afore God, this reverend holy friar,

All our whole city is much bound to him.

JULIET

Nurse, will you go with me into my closet

To help me sort such needful ornaments

As you think fit to furnish me to-morrow?

LADY CAPULET

No, not till Thursday. There is time enough.

CAPULET

Go, Nurse, go with her. We'll to church
    to-morrow.

Exeunt Juliet and Nurse.

LADY CAPULET

We shall be short in our provision.
'Tis now near night.

CAPULET

Tush, I will stir about,
And all things shall be well, I warrant thee, wife.
Go thou to Juliet, help to deck up her.
I'll not to bed to-night; let me alone.
I'll play the housewife for this once. What, ho!

They are all forth; well, I will walk myself
To County Paris, to prepare him up
Against to-morrow. My heart is wondrous light,
Since this same wayward girl is so reclaim'd.

Exeunt.

SCENE III.

JULIET's *chamber.*

Enter JULIET *and* NURSE.

JULIET

Ay, those attires are best; but, gentle nurse,
I pray thee leave me to myself to-night;
For I have need of many orisons
To move the heavens to smile upon my state,
Which, well thou knowest, is cross and full of sin.

Enter LADY CAPULET.

LADY CAPULET

What, are you busy, ho? Need you my help?

JULIET

No, madam; we have cull'd such necessaries

As are behoveful for our state to-morrow.
So please you, let me now be left alone,
And let the nurse this night sit up with you;
For I am sure you have your hands full all
In this so sudden business.

LADY CAPULET
Good night.
Get thee to bed, and rest; for thou hast need.

Exeunt LADY CAPULET *and* NURSE.

JULIET
Farewell! God knows when we shall meet again.
I have a faint cold fear thrills through my veins
That almost freezes up the heat of life.
I'll call them back again to comfort me.
Nurse!—What should she do here?
My dismal scene I needs must act alone.
Come, vial.

What if this mixture do not work at all?

Shall I be married then to-morrow morning?

No, No! This shall forbid it. Lie thou there.

[Lays down a dagger.]

What if it be a poison which the friar

Subtilly hath minist'red to have me dead,

Lest in this marriage he should be dishonour'd

Because he married me before to Romeo?

I fear it is; and yet methinks it should not,

For he hath still been tried a holy man.

I will not entertain so bad a thought.

How if, when I am laid into the tomb,

I wake before the time that Romeo

Come to redeem me? There's a fearful point!

Shall I not then be stifled in the vault,

To whose foul mouth no healthsome air breathes in,

And there die strangled ere my Romeo comes?

Or, if I live, is it not very like

The horrible conceit of death and night,

Together with the terror of the place—

As in a vault, an ancient receptacle

Where for this many hundred years the bones

Of all my buried ancestors are pack'd;

Where bloody Tybalt, yet but green in earth,

Lies fest'ring in his shroud; where, as they say,

At some hours in the night spirits resort—

Alack, alack, is it not like that I,

So early waking—what with loathsome smells,

And shrieks like mandrakes torn out of the earth,

That living mortals, hearing them, run mad—

O, if I wake, shall I not be distraught,

Environed with all these hideous fears,

And madly play with my forefathers' joints,

And pluck the mangled Tybalt from his shroud,

And, in this rage, with some great kinsman's
    bone

As with a club dash out my desp'rate brains?

O, look! methinks I see my cousin's ghost

Seeking out Romeo, that did spit his body

Upon a rapier's point. Stay, Tybalt, stay!

Romeo, I come! this do I drink to thee. *[She drinks and falls upon her bed within the curtains.]*

SCENE IV.

CAPULET'*s house.*

Enter LADY CAPULET *and* NURSE.

LADY CAPULET

Hold, take these keys and fetch more spices, Nurse.

NURSE

They call for dates and quinces in the pastry.

Enter OLD CAPULET.

CAPULET

Come, stir, stir, stir! The second cock hath
    crow'd,
The curfew bell hath rung, 'tis three o'clock.
Look to the bak'd meats, good Angelica;
Spare not for cost.

NURSE

Go, you cot-quean, go,

Get you to bed! Faith, you'll be sick to-morrow

For this night's watching.

CAPULET

No, not a whit. What, I have watch'd ere now

All night for lesser cause, and ne'er been sick.

LADY CAPULET

Ay, you have been a mouse-hunt in your time;

But I will watch you from such watching now.

Exeunt LADY CAPULET *and* NURSE.

CAPULET

A jealous hood, a jealous hood!

Enter three or four SERVINGMEN, *with spits and logs and baskets.*

Now, fellow,
What is there?

FIRST SERVINGMAN
Things for the cook, sir; but I know not what.

CAPULET
Make haste, make haste.

Exit FIRST SERVINGMAN.

Sirrah, fetch drier logs.
Call Peter; he will show thee where they are.

SECOND SERVINGMAN
I have a head, sir, that will find out logs
And never trouble Peter for the matter.

CAPULET

Mass, and well said; a merry whoreson, ha!
Thou shalt be loggerhead.

Exit SECOND SERVINGMAN.

Good faith, 'tis day.
The County will be here with music straight,
For so he said he would. *[Play music.]*
I hear him near.
Nurse! Wife! What, ho! What, Nurse, I say!

Enter NURSE.

Go waken Juliet; go and trim her up.
I'll go and chat with Paris. Hie, make haste,
Make haste! The bridegroom he is come already:
Make haste, I say.

Exeunt.

SCENE V.

JULIET's *chamber.*

Enter NURSE.

NURSE

Mistress! what, mistress! Juliet! Fast, I warrant
    her, she.
Why, lamb! why, lady! Fie, you slug-a-bed!
Why, love, I say! madam! sweetheart! Why, bride!
What, not a word? You take your pennyworths
    now!
Sleep for a week; for the next night, I warrant,
The County Paris hath set up his rest
That you shall rest but little. God forgive me!
Marry, and amen. How sound is she asleep!
I needs must wake her. Madam, madam, madam!
Ay, let the County take you in your bed!
He'll fright you up, i' faith. Will it not be?

[Draws aside the curtains.]

What, dress'd, and in your clothes, and down
   again?
I must needs wake you. Lady! lady! lady!
Alas, alas! Help, help! My lady's dead!
O weraday that ever I was born!
Some aqua vitae, ho! My lord! my lady!

Enter LADY CAPULET.

LADY CAPULET
What noise is here?

NURSE
O lamentable day!

LADY CAPULET
What is the matter?

NURSE

Look, look! O heavy day!

LADY CAPULET

O me, O me! My child, my only life!
Revive, look up, or I will die with thee!
Help, help! Call help.

Enter CAPULET.

CAPULET

For shame, bring Juliet forth; her lord is come.

NURSE

She's dead, deceas'd; she's dead! Alack the day!

LADY CAPULET

Alack the day, she's dead, she's dead, she's dead!

CAPULET

Ha! let me see her. Out alas! she's cold,

Her blood is settled, and her joints are stiff;

Life and these lips have long been separated.

Death lies on her like an untimely frost

Upon the sweetest flower of all the field.

NURSE

O lamentable day!

LADY CAPULET

O woeful time!

CAPULET

Death, that hath ta'en her hence to make me wail,

Ties up my tongue and will not let me speak.

Enter FRIAR LAURENCE *and the* COUNTY PARIS, *with*
MUSICIANS.

FRIAR LAURENCE

Come, is the bride ready to go to church?

CAPULET

Ready to go, but never to return.

O son, the night before thy wedding day

Hath Death lain with thy wife. See, there she lies,

Flower as she was, deflowered by him.

Death is my son-in-law, Death is my heir;

My daughter he hath wedded. I will die

And leave him all. Life, living, all is Death's.

PARIS

Have I thought long to see this morning's face,

And doth it give me such a sight as this?

LADY CAPULET

Accurs'd, unhappy, wretched, hateful day!

Most miserable hour that e'er time saw

In lasting labour of his pilgrimage!

But one, poor one, one poor and loving child,

But one thing to rejoice and solace in,

And cruel Death hath catch'd it from my sight!

Nurse

O woe? O woeful, woeful, woeful day!

Most lamentable day, most woeful day

That ever ever I did yet behold!

O day! O day! O day! O hateful day!

Never was seen so black a day as this.

O woeful day! O woeful day!

Paris

Beguil'd, divorced, wronged, spited, slain!

Most detestable Death, by thee beguil'd,

By cruel cruel thee quite overthrown!

O love! O life! not life, but love in death.

CAPULET

Despis'd, distressed, hated, martyr'd, kill'd!
Uncomfortable time, why cam'st thou now
To murder, murder our solemnity?
O child! O child! my soul, and not my child!
Dead art thou, dead! alack, my child is dead,
And with my child my joys are buried!

FRIAR LAURENCE

Peace, ho, for shame! Confusion's cure lives not
In these confusions. Heaven and yourself
Had part in this fair maid! now heaven hath all,
And all the better is it for the maid.
Your part in her you could not keep from death,
But heaven keeps his part in eternal life.
The most you sought was her promotion,
For 'twas your heaven she should be advanc'd;
And weep ye now, seeing she is advanc'd
Above the clouds, as high as heaven itself?
O, in this love, you love your child so ill
That you run mad, seeing that she is well.

She's not well married that lives married long,
But she's best married that dies married young.
Dry up your tears and stick your rosemary
On this fair corse, and, as the custom is,
In all her best array bear her to church;
For though fond nature bids us all lament,
Yet nature's tears are reason's merriment.

CAPULET

All things that we ordained festival
Turn from their office to black funeral—
Our instruments to melancholy bells,
Our wedding cheer to a sad burial feast;
Our solemn hymns to sullen dirges change;
Our bridal flowers serve for a buried corse;
And all things change them to the contrary.

FRIAR LAURENCE

Sir, go you in; and, madam, go with him;
And go, Sir Paris. Every one prepare

To follow this fair corse unto her grave.

The heavens do low'r upon you for some ill;

Move them no more by crossing their high will.

Exeunt all but MUSICIANS *and* NURSE.

FIRST MUSICIAN

Faith, we may put up our pipes and be gone.

NURSE

Honest good fellows, ah, put up, put up!

For well you know this is a pitiful case.

Exit.

FIRST MUSICIAN

Ay, by my troth, the case may be amended.

Enter PETER.

PETER

Musicians, O, musicians, "Heart's ease," "Heart's
ease"!

O, an you will have me live, play "Heart's ease."

FIRST MUSICIAN

Why "Heart's ease"?

PETER

O, musicians, because my heart itself plays "My
heart is full of woe." O, play me some merry
dump to comfort me.

FIRST MUSICIAN

Not a dump we! 'Tis no time to play now.

PETER

You will not then?

First Musician

No.

Peter

I will then give it you soundly.

First Musician

What will you give us?

Peter

No money, on my faith, but the gleek. I will give you the minstrel.

First Musician

Then will I give you the serving-creature.

PETER

Then will I lay the serving-creature's dagger on
your pate. I will carry no crotchets. I'll re you,
I'll fa you. Do you note me?

FIRST MUSICIAN

An you re us and fa us, you note us.

SECOND MUSICIAN

Pray you put up your dagger, and put out your wit.

PETER

Then have at you with my wit! I will dry-beat
you with an iron wit, and put up my iron dagger.
Answer me like men.

> *When griping grief the heart doth wound,*
> *And doleful dumps the mind oppress,*
> *Then music with her silver sound—*

Why "silver sound"? Why "music with her silver sound"? What say you, Simon Catling?

FIRST MUSICIAN
Marry, sir, because silver hath a sweet sound.

PETER
Pretty! What say you, Hugh Rebeck?

SECOND MUSICIAN
I say "silver sound" because musicians sound for silver.

PETER
Pretty too! What say you, James Soundpost?

THIRD MUSICIAN
Faith, I know not what to say.

PETER

O, I cry you mercy! you are the singer. I will say for you. It is "music with her silver sound" because musicians have no gold for sounding.

> *Then music with her silver sound*
> *With speedy help doth lend redress.*

Exit.

FIRST MUSICIAN

What a pestilent knave is this same?

SECOND MUSICIAN

Hang him, Jack! Come, we'll in here, tarry for the mourners, and stay dinner.

Exeunt.

ACT V

SCENE I.

Enter ROMEO.

ROMEO

If I may trust the flattering truth of sleep
My dreams presage some joyful news at hand.
My bosom's lord sits lightly in his throne,
And all this day an unaccustom'd spirit
Lifts me above the ground with cheerful
   thoughts.
I dreamt my lady came and found me dead
(Strange dream that gives a dead man leave to
   think!)
And breath'd such life with kisses in my lips
That I reviv'd and was an emperor.
Ah me! how sweet is love itself possess'd,
When but love's shadows are so rich in joy!

Enter Romeo's man BALTHASAR, *booted.*

News from Verona! How now, Balthasar?
Dost thou not bring me letters from the friar?
How doth my lady? Is my father well?
How fares my Juliet? That I ask again,
For nothing can be ill if she be well.

BALTHASAR

Then she is well, and nothing can be ill.
Her body sleeps in Capel's monument,
And her immortal part with angels lives.
I saw her laid low in her kindred's vault
And presently took post to tell it you.
O, pardon me for bringing these ill news,
Since you did leave it for my office, sir.

ROMEO

Is it e'en so? Then I defy you, stars!
Thou knowest my lodging. Get me ink and paper
And hire posthorses. I will hence to-night.

BALTHASAR

I do beseech you, sir, have patience.

Your looks are pale and wild and do import

Some misadventure.

ROMEO

Tush, thou art deceiv'd.

Leave me and do the thing I bid thee do.

Hast thou no letters to me from the friar?

BALTHASAR

No, my good lord.

ROMEO

No matter. Get thee gone

And hire those horses. I'll be with thee straight.

Exit Balthasar.

Well, Juliet, I will lie with thee to-night.

Let's see for means. O mischief, thou art swift

To enter in the thoughts of desperate men!
I do remember an apothecary,
And hereabouts 'a dwells, which late I noted
In tatt'red weeds, with overwhelming brows,
Culling of simples. Meager were his looks,
Sharp misery had worn him to the bones;
And in his needy shop a tortoise hung,
An alligator stuff'd, and other skins
Of ill-shaped fishes; and about his shelves
A beggarly account of empty boxes,
Green earthen pots, bladders, and musty seeds,
Remnants of packthread, and old cakes of roses
Were thinly scattered, to make up a show.
Noting this penury, to myself I said,
"An if a man did need a poison now
Whose sale is present death in Mantua,
Here lives a caitiff wretch would sell it him."
O, this same thought did but forerun my need,
And this same needy man must sell it me.
As I remember, this should be the house.
Being holiday, the beggar's shop is shut.
What, ho! apothecary!

Enter APOTHECARY.

APOTHECARY

Who calls so loud?

ROMEO

Come hither, man. I see that thou art poor.

Hold, there is forty ducats. Let me have

A dram of poison, such soon-speeding gear

As will disperse itself through all the veins

That the life-weary taker may fall dead,

And that the trunk may be discharg'd of breath

As violently as hasty powder fir'd

Doth hurry from the fatal cannon's womb.

APOTHECARY

Such mortal drugs I have; but Mantua's law

Is death to any he that utters them.

ROMEO

Art thou so bare and full of wretchedness
And fearest to die? Famine is in thy cheeks,
Need and oppression starveth in thine eyes,
Contempt and beggary hangs upon thy back:
The world is not thy friend, nor the world's law;
The world affords no law to make thee rich;
Then be not poor, but break it and take this.

APOTHECARY

My poverty but not my will consents.

ROMEO

I pay thy poverty and not thy will.

APOTHECARY

Put this in any liquid thing you will
And drink it off, and if you had the strength
Of twenty men, it would dispatch you straight.

Romeo

There is thy gold—worse poison to men's souls,
Doing more murder in this loathsome world,
Than these poor compounds that thou mayst not
    sell.
I sell thee poison; thou hast sold me none.
Farewell. Buy food and get thyself in flesh.
Come, cordial and not poison, go with me
To Juliet's grave; for there must I use thee.

Exeunt.

SCENE II.

VERONA. FRIAR LAURENCE's *cell*.

Enter FRIAR JOHN.

FRIAR JOHN

Holy Franciscan friar, brother, ho!

Enter FRIAR LAURENCE.

FRIAR LAURENCE

This same should be the voice of Friar John
Welcome from Mantua. What says Romeo?
Or, if his mind be writ, give me his letter.

FRIAR JOHN

Going to find a barefoot brother out,
One of our order, to associate me
Here in this city visiting the sick,

And finding him, the searchers of the town,
Suspecting that we both were in a house
Where the infectious pestilence did reign,
Seal'd up the doors, and would not let us forth,
So that my speed to Mantua there was stay'd.

FRIAR LAURENCE
Who bare my letter, then, to Romeo?

FRIAR JOHN
I could not send it—here it is again—
Nor get a messenger to bring it thee,
So fearful were they of infection.

FRIAR LAURENCE
Unhappy fortune! By my brotherhood,
The letter was not nice, but full of charge,
Of dear import; and the neglecting it
May do much danger. Friar John, go hence,

Get me an iron crow and bring it straight
Unto my cell.

FRIAR JOHN
Brother, I'll go and bring it thee.

Exit.

FRIAR LAURENCE
Now, must I to the monument alone.
Within this three hours will fair Juliet wake.
She will beshrew me much that Romeo
Hath had no notice of these accidents;
But I will write again to Mantua,
And keep her at my cell till Romeo come—
Poor living corse, clos'd in a dead man's tomb!

Exit.

SCENE III.

VERONA. *A churchyard; in it the*
monument of the CAPULETS.

Enter PARIS *and his* PAGE *with flowers and a torch.*

PARIS

Give me thy torch, boy. Hence, and stand
  aloof.
Yet put it out, for I would not be seen.
Under yond yew tree lay thee all along,
Holding thine ear close to the hollow ground.
So shall no foot upon the churchyard tread
Being loose, unfirm, with digging up of graves
But thou shalt hear it. Whistle then to me,
As signal that thou hear'st something approach.
Give me those flowers. Do as I bid thee, go.

PAGE

[aside] I am almost afraid to stand alone

Here in the churchyard; yet I will adventure.

[Retires.]

PARIS

Sweet flower, with flowers thy bridal bed I
    strew
(O woe! thy canopy is dust and stones)
Which with sweet water nightly I will dew;
Or, wanting that, with tears distill'd by moans.
The obsequies that I for thee will keep
Nightly shall be to strew thy grave and weep.

[Page whistles.]

The boy gives warning something doth
    approach.
What cursed foot wanders this way to-night
To cross my obsequies and true love's rite?
What, with a torch? Muffle me, night, awhile.

[Retires.]

Enter ROMEO, *and* BALTHASAR *with a torch, a mattock,*
and a crow of iron.

ROMEO
Give me that mattock and the wrenching iron.
Hold, take this letter. Early in the morning
See thou deliver it to my lord and father.
Give me the light. Upon thy life I charge thee,
Whate'er thou hearest or seest, stand all aloof
And do not interrupt me in my course.
Why I descend into this bed of death
Is partly to behold my lady's face,
But chiefly to take thence from her dead finger
A precious ring—a ring that I must use
In dear employment. Therefore hence, be gone.
But if thou, jealous, dost return to pry
In what I farther shall intend to do,
By heaven, I will tear thee joint by joint
And strew this hungry churchyard with thy
    limbs.
The time and my intents are savage-wild,

More fierce and more inexorable far
Than empty tigers or the roaring sea.

BALTHASAR

I will be gone, sir, and not trouble you.

ROMEO

So shalt thou show me friendship. Take thou that.
Live, and be prosperous; and farewell, good
    fellow.

BALTHASAR

[aside] For all this same, I'll hide me hereabout.
His looks I fear, and his intents I doubt. *[Retires.]*

ROMEO

Thou detestable maw, thou womb of death,
Gorg'd with the dearest morsel of the earth,

Thus I enforce thy rotten jaws to open,
And in despite I'll cram thee with more food.

[Romeo opens the tomb.]

PARIS

This is that banish'd haughty Montague
That murd'red my love's cousin—with which grief
It is supposed the fair creature died—
And here is come to do some villainous shame
To the dead bodies. I will apprehend him.

[Comes forward.]

Stop thy unhallowed toil, vile Montague!
Can vengeance be pursu'd further than death?
Condemned villain, I do apprehend thee.
Obey, and go with me; for thou must die.

ROMEO

I must indeed; and therefore came I hither.
Good gentle youth, tempt not a desp'rate man.
Fly hence and leave me. Think upon these gone;

Let them affright thee. I beseech thee, youth,
Put not another sin upon my head
By urging me to fury. O, be gone!
By heaven, I love thee better than myself,
For I come hither arm'd against myself.
Stay not, be gone. Live, and hereafter say
A madman's mercy bid thee run away.

PARIS

I do defy thy conjuration
And apprehend thee for a felon here.

ROMEO

Wilt thou provoke me? Then have at thee, boy!

[They fight.]

PAGE

O Lord, they fight! I will go call the watch.

*Exit. [*PARIS *falls.]*

PARIS

O, I am slain! If thou be merciful,
Open the tomb, lay me with Juliet. *[Dies.]*

ROMEO

In faith, I will. Let me peruse this face.
Mercutio's kinsman, noble County Paris!
What said my man when my betossed soul
Did not attend him as we rode? I think
He told me Paris should have married Juliet.
Said he not so? or did I dream it so?
Or am I mad, hearing him talk of Juliet
To think it was so? O, give me thy hand,
One writ with me in sour misfortune's book!
I'll bury thee in a triumphant grave.
A grave? O, no, a lanthorn, slaught'red youth,
For here lies Juliet, and her beauty makes
This vault a feasting presence full of light.
Death, lie thou there, by a dead man interr'd.

[Lays Paris in the tomb.]

How oft when men are at the point of death
Have they been merry! which their keepers call
A lightning before death. O, how may I
Call this a lightning? O my love! my wife!
Death, that hath suck'd the honey of thy breath,
Hath had no power yet upon thy beauty.
Thou art not conquer'd. Beauty's ensign yet
Is crimson in thy lips and in thy cheeks,
And death's pale flag is not advanced there.
Tybalt, liest thou there in thy bloody sheet?
O, what more favour can I do to thee
Than with that hand that cut thy youth in twain
To sunder his that was thine enemy?
Forgive me, cousin! Ah, dear Juliet,
Why art thou yet so fair? Shall I believe
That unsubstantial Death is amorous,
And that the lean abhorred monster keeps
Thee here in dark to be his paramour?
For fear of that I still will stay with thee
And never from this palace of dim night
Depart again. Here, here will I remain
With worms that are thy chambermaids. O, here

Will I set up my everlasting rest
And shake the yoke of inauspicious stars
From this world-wearied flesh. Eyes, look your
    last!
Arms, take your last embrace! and, lips, O you
The doors of breath, seal with a righteous kiss
A dateless bargain to engrossing death!
Come, bitter conduct; come, unsavoury guide!
Thou desperate pilot, now at once run on
The dashing rocks thy seasick weary bark!
Here's to my love! *[Drinks.]* O true apothecary!
Thy drugs are quick. Thus with a kiss I die.
    [Falls.]

Enter Friar Laurence, *with lanthorn, crow, and spade.*

Friar Laurence

Saint Francis be my speed! how oft to-night
Have my old feet stumbled at graves! Who's
    there?

BALTHASAR

Here's one, a friend, and one that knows you well.

FRIAR LAURENCE

Bliss be upon you! Tell me, good my friend,
What torch is yond that vainly lends his light
To grubs and eyeless skulls? As I discern,
It burneth in the Capels' monument.

BALTHASAR

It doth so, holy sir; and there's my master,
One that you love.

FRIAR LAURENCE

Who is it?

BALTHASAR

Romeo.

FRIAR LAURENCE
How long hath he been there?

BALTHASAR
Full half an hour.

FRIAR LAURENCE
Go with me to the vault.

BALTHASAR
I dare not, sir.
My master knows not but I am gone hence,
And fearfully did menace me with death
If I did stay to look on his intents.

FRIAR LAURENCE
Stay then; I'll go alone. Fear comes upon me.
O, much I fear some ill unthrifty thing.

BALTHASAR

As I did sleep under this yew tree here,
I dreamt my master and another fought,
And that my master slew him.

FRIAR LAURENCE

Romeo!
Alack, alack, what blood is this which stains
The stony entrance of this sepulchre?
What mean these masterless and gory swords
To lie discolour'd by this place of peace?

[Enters the tomb.]

Romeo! O, pale! Who else? What, Paris too?
And steep'd in blood? Ah, what an unkind hour
Is guilty of this lamentable chance! The lady
   stirs.

[Juliet rises.]

JULIET

O comfortable friar! where is my lord?
I do remember well where I should be,
And there I am. Where is my Romeo?

[Noise within.]

FRIAR LAURENCE

I hear some noise. Lady, come from that nest
Of death, contagion, and unnatural sleep.
A greater power than we can contradict
Hath thwarted our intents. Come, come away.
Thy husband in thy bosom there lies dead;
And Paris too. Come, I'll dispose of thee
Among a sisterhood of holy nuns.
Stay not to question, for the watch is coming.
Come, go, good Juliet. I dare no longer stay.

JULIET

Go, get thee hence, for I will not away.

Exit FRIAR LAURENCE.

What's here? A cup, clos'd in my true love's
    hand?
Poison, I see, hath been his timeless end.
O churl! drunk all, and left no friendly drop
To help me after? I will kiss thy lips.
Haply some poison yet doth hang on them
To make me die with a restorative. *[Kisses him.]*
Thy lips are warm!

FIRST WATCHMAN

[within] Lead, boy. Which way?

JULIET

Yea, noise? Then I'll be brief. O happy dagger!

[Snatches Romeo's dagger.]

This is thy sheath; there rest, and let me die.

[She stabs herself and falls on ROMEO's body.]

Enter PARIS' PAGE *and* WATCHMEN.

BOY

This is the place. There, where the torch doth
    burn.

FIRST WATCHMAN

The ground is bloody. Search about the
    churchyard.
Go, some of you; whoe'er you find attach.

                            Exeunt some Watchmen.

Pitiful sight! here lies the County slain;
And Juliet bleeding, warm, and newly dead,
Who here hath lain this two days buried.
Go, tell the Prince; run to the Capulets;
Raise up the Montagues; some others search.

                            Exeunt other Watchmen.

We see the ground whereon these woes do lie,
But the true ground of all these piteous woes
We cannot without circumstance descry.

Enter some Watchmen, with Romeo's man BALTHASAR.

SECOND WATCHMAN

Here's Romeo's man.
We found him in the churchyard.

FIRST WATCHMAN

Hold him in safety till the Prince come hither.

Enter FRIAR LAURENCE *and another* WATCHMAN.

THIRD WATCHMAN

Here is a friar that trembles, sighs, and weeps.
We took this mattock and this spade from him
As he was coming from this churchyard side.

FIRST WATCHMAN

A great suspicion! Stay the friar too.

Enter the PRINCE *and attendants.*

PRINCE

What misadventure is so early up,

That calls our person from our morning
  rest?

Enter CAPULET *and* LADY CAPULET *with others.*

CAPULET

What should it be, that they so shriek abroad?

LADY CAPULET

The people in the street cry "Romeo,"

Some "Juliet," and some "Paris"; and all run,

With open outcry, toward our monument.

PRINCE
What fear is this which startles in our ears?

FIRST WATCHMAN
Sovereign, here lies the County Paris slain;
And Romeo dead; and Juliet, dead before,
Warm and new kill'd.

PRINCE
Search, seek, and know how this foul murder
  comes.

FIRST WATCHMAN
Here is a friar, and slaughter'd Romeo's man,
With instruments upon them fit to open
These dead men's tombs.

William Shakespeare

CAPULET

O heavens! O wife, look how our daughter
  bleeds!
This dagger hath mista'en, for, lo, his house
Is empty on the back of Montague,
And it missheathed in my daughter's bosom!

LADY CAPULET

O me! this sight of death is as a bell
That warns my old age to a sepulchre.

Enter MONTAGUE *and others.*

PRINCE

Come, Montague; for thou art early up
To see thy son and heir more early down.

MONTAGUE

Alas, my liege, my wife is dead to-night!

Grief of my son's exile hath stopp'd her breath.

What further woe conspires against mine age?

PRINCE

Look, and thou shalt see.

MONTAGUE

O thou untaught! what manners is in this,

To press before thy father to a grave?

PRINCE

Seal up the mouth of outrage for a while,

Till we can clear these ambiguities

And know their spring, their head, their true

    descent;

And then will I be general of your woes

And lead you even to death. Meantime forbear,

And let mischance be slave to patience.

Bring forth the parties of suspicion.

Friar Laurence

I am the greatest, able to do least,
Yet most suspected, as the time and place
Doth make against me, of this direful murder;
And here I stand, both to impeach and purge
Myself condemned and myself excus'd.

Prince

Then say it once what thou dost know in this.

Friar Laurence

I will be brief, for my short date of breath
Is not so long as is a tedious tale.
Romeo, there dead, was husband to that Juliet;
And she, there dead, that Romeo's faithful wife.
I married them; and their stol'n marriage day
Was Tybalt's doomsday, whose untimely death
Banish'd the new-made bridegroom from this city;
For whom, and not for Tybalt, Juliet pin'd.
You, to remove that siege of grief from her,

Betroth'd and would have married her perforce

To County Paris. Then comes she to me

And with wild looks bid me devise some mean

To rid her from this second marriage,

Or in my cell there would she kill herself.

Then gave I her (so tutored by my art)

A sleeping potion; which so took effect

As I intended, for it wrought on her

The form of death. Meantime I writ to Romeo

That he should hither come as this dire night

To help to take her from her borrowed grave,

Being the time the potion's force should cease.

But he which bore my letter, Friar John,

Was stay'd by accident, and yesternight

Return'd my letter back. Then all alone

At the prefixed hour of her waking

Came I to take her from her kindred's vault;

Meaning to keep her closely at my cell

Till I conveniently could send to Romeo.

But when I came, some minute ere the time

Of her awaking, here untimely lay

The noble Paris and true Romeo dead.

She wakes; and I entreated her come forth
And bear this work of heaven with patience;
But then a noise did scare me from the tomb,
And she, too desperate, would not go with me,
But, as it seems, did violence on herself.
All this I know, and to the marriage
Her nurse is privy; and if aught in this
Miscarried by my fault, let my old life
Be sacrific'd, some hour before his time,
Unto the rigour of severest law.

PRINCE
We still have known thee for a holy man.
Where's Romeo's man? What can he say in this?

BALTHASAR
I brought my master news of Juliet's death;
And then in post he came from Mantua
To this same place, to this same monument.
This letter he early bid me give his father,

And threat'ned me with death, going in the vault,
If I departed not and left him there.

> **PRINCE**
> Give me the letter. I will look on it.
> Where is the County's page that rais'd the watch?
> Sirrah, what made your master in this place?

> **PAGE**
> He came with flowers to strew his lady's grave;
> And bid me stand aloof, and so I did.
> Anon comes one with light to ope the tomb;
> And by-and-by my master drew on him;
> And then I ran away to call the watch.

> **PRINCE**
> This letter doth make good the friar's words,
> Their course of love, the tidings of her death;
> And here he writes that he did buy a poison

Of a poor 'pothecary, and therewithal
Came to this vault to die, and lie with Juliet.
Where be these enemies? Capulet, Montague,
See what a scourge is laid upon your hate,
That heaven finds means to kill your joys with
    love!
And I, for winking at you, discords too,
Have lost a brace of kinsmen. All are punish'd.

CAPULET

O brother Montague, give me thy hand.
This is my daughter's jointure, for no more
Can I demand.

MONTAGUE

But I can give thee more;
For I will raise her Statue in pure gold,
That whiles Verona by that name is known,
There shall no figure at such rate be set
As that of true and faithful Juliet.

CAPULET

As rich shall Romeo's by his lady's lie—
Poor sacrifices of our enmity!

PRINCE

A glooming peace this morning with it brings.
The sun for sorrow will not show his head.
Go hence, to have more talk of these sad things;
Some shall be pardon'd, and some punished;
For never was a story of more woe
Than this of Juliet and her Romeo.

Exeunt omnes.

Romeo & Juliet

Quiz: What would you do in the name of love? Find out how you measure up against Shakespeare's timeless lovers!

Test Yourself: How much do you know about the star-crossed lovers? Take this quiz!

10 Things You Didn't Know About William Shakespeare

What if Romeo and Juliet lived now and were on Facebook?

Quiz:
What would you do in the name of love? Find out how you measure up against Shakespeare's timeless lovers!

1. Your boyfriend wants to go see the newest action flick this Thursday, but you usually have dinner with your girlfriends on Thursday nights. You
   a. ditch your friends. You have dinner every Thursday. They won't miss you this once.
   b. tell your boyfriend you'll go on Friday, but Thursday nights are sacred.
   c. invite your guy along for dinner, and tell him if there's a late showing you'd be up for it.

2. Your crush's birthday is coming up. You've liked him for a year, but as far as you know, he just sees you as a fun friend. On his birthday, you
   a. make sure to pass by his locker in between classes and give him a big smile and a "happy birthday!"
   b. make him a mix CD of some of your favorite new songs and wink at him as you unzip the front of his backpack to stick it in.
   c. camp out on his front lawn to serenade him as he leaves for school. You've spent the past month learning how to play his favorite song on the acoustic guitar.

3. It's spring of senior year, and you just received a nice big pile of college acceptances. You got into

your dream school with a full scholarship, but your boyfriend unfortunately did not. Now what?

   a. College is college, right? We can just go to the state school we both got into.

   b. Um, there's no way I'm passing up my dream acceptance and all that money for my boyfriend. We can visit on holidays.

   c. I'll talk to my boyfriend about applying to the rolling admissions state school that's near my dream college. Either way, things will work out the way they're supposed to.

4. Your boyfriend wants to whisk you away for a romantic weekend vacation, but you've already promised your parents and little sister that you'd go with them on the family beach vacation. What do you do?

   a. Ditch the 'rents. Family vacation would have been boring anyway.

   b. If the weekend getaway is in Paris or Tahiti, you'll go with your boyfriend—can't miss out on an opportunity like that! But otherwise, you'd feel guilty going back on family plans.

   c. Tell him sorry, family comes first. Another time.

5. The guy you've been dating is away on a school trip and won't be back for a couple of days. Because you miss him, you

   a. listen to the songs that remind you of him . . .

EXTRAS

and then listen to some happy songs since all this moping is making you depressed.

b. spend extra time hanging out with your friends and just generally keeping busy.

c. head over to his house to hang out with his family. Being around them really reminds you of him.

6. You go out for a nice dinner to celebrate your one-year anniversary with your boyfriend, and he presents you with a telltale little teal box with white ribbon. When you open it to discover a huge ring inside, you

a. freak out. That is so not appropriate at this age. And where did he get the money for this?

b. secretly love it, but make a few wisecracks about not getting married young just so he knows that you won't be ready for anything like that anytime soon.

c. shriek and then kiss him, wishing desperately the box had been accompanied by a certain significant question.

Key: 1. a=3, b=1, c=2. 2. a=1, b=2, c=3. 3. a=3, b=1, c=2. 4. a=3, b=2, c=1. 5. a=2, b=1, c=3. 6. a=1, b=2, c=3.

If you got . . .

6–9 points:
You're a sensible, cheerful person. You have definite priorities in life, and you're wise enough not to let boys come between you and your family, your friends, and your goals. But be careful that you aren't being too sensible—make sure your guy knows that you like him! Being impulsive every once in a while isn't the end of the world, and who knows, you might make some amazing memories.

10–13 points:
Sometimes you're emotional and impulsive, but you usually see reason when making big decisions. You're pretty balanced in your relationships. Good for you! Just make sure you're seeing straight when important decisions come your way—just think of what happened to Romeo and Juliet because of hasty actions.

14–18 points:
You're a true romantic. You feel everything very deeply, and you don't understand people who don't make sacrifices for love. Juliet and her lover Romeo would commend you on your loyalty and passion. But be careful; remember what happened when they sacrificed everything for love. Make sure you're well informed before making any drastic decisions!

Test Yourself:
How much do you know about the star-crossed lovers?
Take this quiz!

1. The original story of Romeo and Juliet can be traced back to:
   a. an age-old Italian tradition of tragic romances
   b. "The Tragical History of Romeus and Juliet" by Arthur Brooke
   c. Shakespeare's play from the end of the sixteenth century
   d. MGM's 1936 movie *Romeo and Juliet*

2. *Romeo and Juliet* has since been transformed into:
   a. a movie
   b. an opera
   c. a ballet
   d. a musical
   e. all of the above

3. Which of the following actors was NOT in Baz Luhrmann's 1996 movie *Romeo + Juliet*?
   a. Paul Rudd
   b. Leonardo DiCaprio
   c. Hank Azaria
   d. Jesse Bradford

4. Which famous quotation is NOT from *Romeo and Juliet*?
   a. "But soft! What light through yonder window

breaks? It is the east . . ."

b. "O true apothecary! Thy drugs are quick. Thus with a kiss I die."

c. "What's in a name? That which we call a rose by any other name would smell as sweet."

d. "Tomorrow, and tomorrow, and tomorrow, creeps in this petty pace from day to day. . . ."

5. Which of the following is FALSE?

a. The full title of Shakespeare's play is *The Most Excellent and Lamentable Tragedy of Romeo and Juliet.*

b. Juliet is meant to be about seventeen years old when she meets Romeo in the play.

c. Because women were not allowed to be actors in the sixteenth century, Juliet would have been portrayed by a man in the original productions.

d. There are more than seventy film versions and adaptations of the play.

Answer Key:

1: **Both A and B**. Many of Shakespeare's plots are new versions of traditional stories that have been passed down for generations, and they often owe quite a bit to previous written versions of the story as well. While Shakespeare's plots are predominantly not his own, his language and his deft portraits of his characters are what make him a celebrated playwright.

2: **E**. This story has reappeared as a Baz Luhrmann film starring Leonardo DiCaprio, a well-loved musical by Sondheim and Bernstein (*West Side Story*), a famous ballet by Prokofiev, and much more. Audiences never seem to get tired of the star-crossed lovers!

3: **C**. Hank Azaria. Rudd and Bradford played supporting roles in the film; DiCaprio famously portrayed Romeo himself.

4: **D**. This is the beginning of a famous speech from Shakespeare's tragedy *Macbeth*.

5: **B**. Juliet is actually intended to be thirteen, a fact that is rarely reflected in casting choices for movie or stage productions.

10 Things You Didn't Know About William Shakespeare

1. Shakespeare was born in 1564. Shakespeare was the third child of eight in his family. His father was a middle-class citizen who served in town government, but after a steadily successful career he ran up large debts and was removed from office.

2. Shakespeare got married in 1582, when he was only eighteen—to Anne Hathaway, a woman eight years older than he was. (Perhaps she was an ancestor of Anne Hathaway, star of *The Princess Diaries*?)

3. It might seem scandalous to us to discover that Anne was pregnant at the time of their marriage, but in fact about a third of Renaissance women were pregnant at the time of marriage. Many Renaissance couples had a "handfasting" ceremony promising themselves to each other long before actually marrying; in cases like these, pregnancies before marriage were not unusual. We don't know for sure whether William Shakespeare and Anne Hathaway performed this kind of betrothal ceremony before Anne became pregnant.

4. Mysteriously, Shakespeare left his home and his family behind to find his fortune only four years after getting married.

5. Almost nothing is known about the years between

EXTRAS

Shakespeare's departure from Stratford-upon-Avon and his first moments of recognition as an accomplished playwright in London nearly a decade later. These years are known as the "lost years" and are often thought to be the time that Shakespeare gained experience and wisdom about the world before showing up in the theater world in London.

6. Less than ten years after leaving home, Shakespeare had made enough of a name for himself to become a senior member of an acting company called the Lord Chamberlain's Men. This group later became a royal company, making Shakespeare an official playwright to the king!

7. Shakespeare was very successful during his lifetime, unlike some writers. His family was granted a coat of arms, making him a certified "gentleman." He bought a good deal of property, and he also became partial owner of the Globe Theatre, the famous theater where many of his plays were performed.

8. Shakespeare was the father of three children: Susanna, Hamnet, and Judith. Hamnet died for unknown reasons at the age of eleven.

9. In 1593, many theaters had to be shut down because there was a terrible London outbreak of the bubonic plague, the disease also known as the Black Death. This epidemic killed more than 10,000 London

residents during the 1593 outbreak alone.

10. Shakespeare died of unknown causes in 1616. Although we don't know why he died, we do have his will, which strangely mentions his wife, Anne, only to give her his "second best" bed. This is seen by many to have been a slight to her, or even a sign of an unhappy marriage. Of course, at the time she would automatically have rights to a third of his estate, even without his explicit acknowledgment.

Sources: Absolute Shakespeare online:
http://absoluteshakespeare.com/william_shakespeare.htm
Shakespeare's life and times:
http://shakespeare.palomar.edu/life.htm
Shakespeare 4 Kidz:
http://www.shakespeare4kidz.com/romeo-and-juliet-facts-and-trivia.html
PBS:
http://www.pbs.org/shakespeare/events/event115.html

What if Romeo and Juliet lived now and had Facebook?

Name: Romeo M.
Sex: Male
Hometown: Verona
Relationship status: Engaged to Juliet C.
Interested in: Women
Looking for: Friendship, Dating, A Relationship
Political views: Liberal
Religious views: Catholic
Activities: going to dances, kissing,
talking, hanging with Mercutio
Interests: Juliet, love, poetry, kissing, letting lips
do what hands do (in holy palmer's kiss)
Favorite music: Radiohead, *West Side Story* soundtrack, *Moulin Rouge!* soundtrack, "Kissing You" by Des'ree, Death Cab For Cutie
Favorite TV shows: *One Tree Hill, Smallville, Degrassi*, old *Dawson's Creek* episodes
Favorite movies: *Moulin Rouge!, The Notebook, Shakespeare in Love, Atonement, 10 Things I Hate About You, Fight Club, Ferris Bueller's Day Off*
About Me:
These are my firsts. If I tag you it means I want to know yours. Copy and paste this note into your notes, delete my answers, and fill yours in. Tag me back and anyone else whose "firsts" you want to know about. . . .
Some of these are kind of embarrassing, guys, so don't make fun of me, LOL

1. Who was your FIRST prom date?
Rosaline . . . but it was totally arranged by my parents, like my WHOLE LIFE is.

2. Do you still talk to your FIRST love?
No . . . after prom she told me she didn't want to date me anymore. It's okay, it wasn't really love anyways, which I know now.

3. What was your FIRST alcoholic drink?
Wine. My family always has red wine with dinner. This is before Verona had a drinking age, though. (duh)

4. What was your FIRST job?
Don't have a job . . . although I want to be a poet!

5. What was your FIRST car?
Mustang

6. Who was the FIRST person to text/IM you today?
Mercutio. The jerk woke me up at 5 a.m.

7. Who is the FIRST person you thought of this morning?
Juliet

8. Where did you go on your FIRST ride on an airplane?
Italy

9. Who was your FIRST best friend?
Mercutio (don't tell Benvolio)

10. Who was the FIRST person you talked to today?
Dad at breakfast

11. Whose wedding were you in the FIRST time?
My cousin's

12. What was the FIRST thing you did this morning?
Texted Mercutio about the weird dream I had last night.
He's good at analyzing that crap.

13. What was the FIRST concert you ever went to?
Celine Dion (dude, you know you loved "My Heart Will Go On")

14. FIRST tattoo?
Don't have one yet but I want to get Juliet's name . . . not telling where.

15. FIRST piercing?
None

16. FIRST movie you remember seeing?
Casablanca . . . or like *Beauty and the Beast*

17. When was your FIRST detention?
I don't really go to school.

18. What is something you would learn if you had the chance?
How to be patient. I'm so impulsive. LOL

19. Did you marry the FIRST person to ask for your hand in marriage?
Nope—the first person who I asked, yep!

20. What was the FIRST sport that you were involved in?
Fencing

21. What were the FIRST lessons you ever took?
Latin, Greek, fencing, dancing . . . okay, I sound like a loser.

22. What is the FIRST thing you do when you get home?
Eat dinner in my room and write my blog

23. Where did you go on your FIRST date?
Well, I guess Juls & my first date was at this dance. . . . I was really nervous and also her family was watching so we couldn't really talk. But we definitely knew we liked each other right away, and I even danced with her a little.

Name: Juliet C.
Sex: Female
Hometown: Verona
Relationship status: Engaged to Romeo M.
Interested in: Men
Looking for: Friendship
Political views: Moderate
Religious views: Catholic
Activities: shopping, going to the beach with my nurse, reading poetry, going to parties, going to church
Interests: Romeo M., true love, passion, flowers, beauty, life
Favorite music: Prokofiev, Brahms, Debussy, James Blunt, Sixpence None the Richer, Jason Mraz, Natasha Bedingfield, Sara Bareilles, Mariah Carey (she's really good, guys!)
Favorite TV shows: *Sex and the City, Degrassi, What Not To Wear, Gossip Girl, The Secret Life of the American Teenager*
Favorite movies: *Titanic, Garden State, You've Got Mail, When Harry Met Sally, Love Actually, Harry Potter, 27 Dresses, The Proposal, Twilight*

About Me:

I got this quiz from Romeo (I <3 you, Roms!) and it was awesome!!! You all should fill it out, too! These are my firsts. If I tag you it means I want to know yours. Copy and paste this note into your notes, delete my answers, and fill yours in. Tag me back and anyone else whose "firsts" you want to know about. . . .

1. Who was your FIRST prom date?
My parents say I'm too young to go to prom. :-(

2. Do you still talk to your FIRST love?
We're engaged, hello!

3. What was your FIRST alcoholic drink?
My family has wine with dinner but they usually water mine down. . . . I don't really like it.

4. What was your FIRST job?
I'm just a daughter and a student, I guess.

5. What was your FIRST car?
Don't have one but my daddy drives a Benz.

6. Who was the FIRST person to text/IM you today?
Romeo <3 he texted me to say good morning. He's so sweet.

7. Who is the FIRST person you thought of this morning?
Romeo, duh

8. Where did you go on your FIRST ride on an airplane?
Italy

9. Who was your FIRST best friend?
My nurse

10. Who was the FIRST person you talked to today?
Nurse when she brought my delicious breakfast for me!

11. Whose wedding were you in the FIRST time?
Haven't been in one yet, but soon I'll be the STAR of one!

12. What was the FIRST thing you did this morning?
Took a long bath, fixed my hair, picked out my clothes for the day

13. What was the FIRST concert you ever went to?
Probably a concert violinist or something

14. FIRST tattoo?
Ew! I HATE tattoos. Good thing Romeo doesn't have any.

15. FIRST piercing?
My ears

16. FIRST movie you remember seeing?
The Little Mermaid. I love that movie.

17. When was your FIRST detention?
My nurse homeschools me, so I get grounded instead of getting detention.

18. What is something you would learn if you had the chance?
How to be better at communicating. People say I'm really secretive and that they never know what I'm planning.

19. Did you marry the FIRST person to ask for your hand in marriage?
Well, Paris tried to ask for my hand, but I wouldn't really let him. I'm glad Romeo asked next, because now we're actually going to get married!!!

20. What was the FIRST sport that you were involved in?
Does dancing count?

21. What were the FIRST lessons you ever took?
Dancing, cooking, sewing, French

22. What is the I FIRST thing you do when you get home?
Tell my nurse all about my day . . . well, everything that isn't private, of course.

23. Where did you go on your FIRST date?
I don't know if this counts, but Romeo and I met at this party my family was having. It was kind of awkward and he's not really that great of a dancer (Romeo, I hope you aren't reading this!!! LOL), but it was soooo romantic anyway.